Of Love and Death
and Other Journeys

Also by Isabelle Holland

Heads You Win, Tails I Lose

The Man Without a Face

Amanda's Choice

Cecily

Of Love and Death and Other Journeys

by Isabelle Holland

J. B. Lippincott Company | Philadelphia and New York

U.S. Library of Congress Cataloging in Publication Data

Holland, Isabelle.
  Of love and death and other journeys.

  SUMMARY: Meg Grant's sixteenth year is a time of love and loss and new understanding.
  [1. Italy—Fiction. 2. Parent and child—Fiction. 3. Death—Fiction] I. Title.
PL7.H7083Of [Fic]   74-30012
ISBN 0-397-31566-X

For Ursula, again

with thanks

1

I met my father for the first time when I was fifteen. It happened like this. Mother and Peter and I had just arrived at Cotton's cottage outside Perugia for our summer stint with the tourists. Our operation was not one of the better-known guide outfits owing to such irritating details as not having a permanent reliable car (our car was permanent but not reliable), no money for advertising and Mother's tendency not to be able to tell the difference between a Botticelli and a Raphael.

"It puts people off," Peter said indignantly, when some female from the prairie states had complained about Mother's little mistake over one of Raphael's better-known canvases. "They feel they're not getting their money's worth."

Mother was, as always, unrepentant. "That woman wouldn't know the difference between a painting and a paint rag. She should be grateful I pointed it out."

Peter sighed and we were all quiet for a moment. It wasn't that we were being critical of Mother. It had just been awkward to scrounge up the seven thousand lire the irate customer had demanded back. Cotton had produced (reluctantly) four thousand and Peter had pawned his watch again.

"Next time," Cotton said, all but kissing the thousand-lira notes as he handed them over one by one, "take Mopsy with you." He pulled my hair. "She may not be very couth, but she knows a Giotto from a Perugino."

Cotton's real name was Andrew MacKenzie. He was a painter. In winter he lived in Perugia and taught English at the university there. In summer he moved himself, his easel, his canvases and his other shirt to a former peasants' farmhouse more or less midway between Perugia and Florence. The house was on the property of the late Conte di Renaldi. The contessa, originally from Boston, had decided to improve the family's diminishing fortunes by renovating some of the peasants' farmhouses, now that the peasants had all left for the big city, and renting them at extortionate prices to Americans and rich northern Europeans who came to soak up sun and culture. Cotton's house was one of the unrenovated ones, so it still smelled of goat and chickens and had a tin bathtub, one faucet and an ancient wheezing toilet that sometimes actually worked. The rest of the time we kept buckets of water handy to pour down what Peter called "the loo" to aid the tired and aging water pressure.

"If you would occasionally leave your masterpieces," Mother said rather bitterly to Cotton when the incident of the Raphael occurred in Florence, "this wouldn't have happened. I've never pretended to be an art connoisseur. I supply the gossip, the anecdotes, the little touches that make our guided tours memorable, different—"

"They're different, all right," Cotton agreed. "As I said, next time take Mops. Otherwise no more money." He grinned at me.

Cotton was six feet two inches, twenty-nine years old and had red hair and beard. I'd been in love with him since I could remember and had made up my mind to marry him when I got a bit older. By a bit older, I meant maybe eighteen, at which point he'd be thirty-two.

Mother leaned over and gave me a big hug. "I'm always happy to take Mopsy. Aren't I, love?"

I returned the hug and Mother squeaked. "Watch out for my ribs! Mops, you don't think you're still growing, do you?"

"God forbid!" That was Peter Smith, Mother's present husband. He was lying on Cotton's sofa, the one without any springs. He was shortish, fattish and fairish. And whenever he was lying down or staring into space, which was a large part of the time, he said he was working

9

on the plot of his new book. Peter wrote borderline pornography for some French firm that kept going out of business largely, Cotton claimed, because their pornography lacked conviction.

"You have to believe that kind of stuff," Cotton said, when the last publisher's check bounced, "or it doesn't work. Or so I'm told, anyway."

"True," Peter sighed. "I lack dedication. I suppose it's because I can't think of it as my real vocation. Just a means." What Peter really wanted to do was write the definitive book on canon law in the twelfth century. But, as he said, while the world was undoubtedly waiting for this scholarly volume, it was waiting with unending patience. No one, so far, had rushed forward with the kind of advance that would enable The Pride to live for the two or three years necessary while Peter got up his footnotes. The Pride was us: Mother, me, Andrew (sometimes) and Peter, otherwise known as Flopsy, Mopsy, Cottontail and Peter. My real name is Margaret. Mother's is Phoebe. But because she ran to freckles and had a passion for large, floppy leghorn straw hats, the first time Cotton saw her he called her Flopsy. Being as how she was married to someone named Peter, the rest of the names followed as a matter of course. Peter was English. Mother and I were American. Andrew was half and half.

"It beats me," Mother said, "where Mopsy gets her learning. It isn't as though she'd ever really gone to school."

Cotton narrowed his eyes and looked at the tawny

landscape of his painting. "She has natural talent. Much better than school."

We all agreed heartily. School for me was a sore subject. I had been to quite a few in Mother's vagabond meanderings. I had been to school (for brief periods) in Italy, France, Belgium, England, Spain, Germany and Switzerland. I could speak five languages well enough to conduct an argument or buy food. I knew the Umbrian school of painters the way kids in America knew baseball scores. I didn't know algebra from an abacus, but I could recite the opening lines of Dante's *Inferno* and all the sovereigns of England since the Norman Conquest. On the other hand when, a few years ago, a suspicious American consul asked who delivered the Gettysburg Address, I said it was George Washington.

"I thought you said she was being tutored," the consul said sternly to Mother.

"She's a little backward," Mother replied in a whisper. "It's quite tragic."

I tried to look as backward as possible while the consul stared at me. "I see," he said drily. "And what does her father—er—think of this—er—state of affairs?"

"He's dead," Mother said, and groped for her handkerchief.

"You never told me Father was dead," I said, when we emerged from the consulate. "Is he?"

"Not entirely," Mother conceded. "Just from the neck up."

Father was Alan Fraser Grant VI. He and Mother had split up when I was on the way and he had never shown the faintest interest in me since. It was at the beginning of the past summer when I suffered my annual upsurge of interest in Father, brought on by our encounter with the first wave of American tourists, that I asked my yearly question, not really expecting an answer that would tell me anything. On the subject of Father, Mother was always maddeningly vague.

"What's Father really like?" I asked, *à propos* of nothing, as we were having a snack before meeting some tourists. I think I was working on the principle that an ambush approach might produce something definite for a change.

Mother said gloomily, "A stuffed shirt. And when I say stuffed, I mean crammed."

"Crammed with what?"

"Stupid, outmoded, old-fashioned, exploded ideas."

"Such as?"

"Such as a woman's place is in the home."

"Oh." I could see where an attitude like that could make serious difficulties for Father. "You'd think," I finally said, coming out with my real grievance against him, "that he'd at least want to see me. Out of curiosity alone, if nothing else."

"Curiosity is vulgar. I know, because all the Grants since the flood have thought so. They told me."

"Do they really go back that far? To the flood?"

Mother looked at me over her *limon pressé* at a table on

the Corso, the main street in Perugia. "It's not generally known, but the Grants *caused* the flood in order to purge the world of people who showed vulgar attitudes like curiosity."

We then both giggled.

"I still think, though," I said, worrying at my grievance, "that even though he's a Grant and therefore a stuffed shirt, he'd want to see me."

"Yes, you would, wouldn't you? Come along, Meg. Drink your Coke or orange or whatever and let's be moving. We have to meet the new batch of Goodies at the museum." Goodies were tourists.

So we paid our discounted bill and promised Sergio, the manager, that we would drive our flock past his restaurant at the psychological moment when their feet were giving out and their minds were glazed and their stomachs were empty. As we made our way to the museum I wondered what I'd said or done to annoy Mother, because she only called me Meg when she was annoyed with me. Then as I saw our Goodies, almost invisible behind cameras, waiting for us at the big doors of the museum, I forgot about it. As Peter once said, there was no point in trying to figure out what Mother thought and why. One accepted her with joy as an Act of God.

But when I looked back on it afterwards, that was the day that started the process that brought Father and me together. It was memorable for two events. The first was merely funny—at least it was to Mother and me and the non-American members of our Goodie Pack. Mother, standing in front of a glowing painting by Il Perugino, had

13

just finished her speech about this fifteenth-century painter who was known by the name of his native town, Perugia, and naturally given pride of place in the museum, when, after a respectful silence, an unmistakably Midwestern voice spoke up from the back of the little huddle we had collected.

"Is that an original?"

All the English, Canadians and other assorted English-speaking types within hearing looked delighted at this gaffe. It simply confirmed their view of Americans.

All the other Americans groaned and then turned with bared teeth to rend their countrywoman who had disgraced them.

Mother put her hand up to her mouth and smothered a giggle. Her hazel eyes danced. I remember looking down on her from my seven inches of superior height and when I close my eyes I can see her again at that moment—the reddish sandy curls escaping from her big hat, her yellow dress, the impish look on her face, the marvelous painting to one side—because though I didn't know it then, something in my life had started to come to an end.

The second event happened just as we were leaving the museum around twelve thirty. The Goodies were streaming out ahead onto the Corso, hungry, footsore and desperately in need of sustenance, just as Mother and I knew they would be, and still sending infuriated looks at the poor woman from Kansas or Iowa or Missouri.

"Let me explain—" she was saying tearfully.

Mother, her hand still on the heavy stone banister at

the foot of the staircase, said, "I know a place . . ." And then she stopped.

"What's the matter?" I asked. "Don't tell me we've left a Goodie upstairs or in the ladies' room?" (That had happened once before.)

"Meg . . ." Mother said.

I waited, and then when she didn't say anything more I moved back towards her. It was dark there in the cool stone corridor, but I decided Mother looked funny. That is, she looked her age, which was thirty-five. Usually she looked about twenty-three and I'd twice been with her when she had to produce identification to prove she was over twenty-one.

"Have you got The Blight again?" I asked. The Blight was what Mother called, with great dignity, "my nervous stomach." Peter, being English, called it "a touch of liver." Cotton—who, Mother said, always looks at things in the worst possible way—called it a hangover. Mother said this was impossible as she did not drink hard liquor, but there was no getting around the fact that she and Peter had what Cotton described as a dedicated and devoted approach to the *vin du pays*, and they had made tremendous inroads on some bottles of wine the previous evening.

"I have some soda tablets with me," I said, ever Miss Helpful. When one escorts tourists one travels equipped for anything.

Mother let out her breath and said, "I'm all right," and started towards the door. I saw her face, then, and it was as though I were looking at a stranger. The grown-up child I had always known as my mother was gone. In her place was a pasty-faced woman with nondescript features.

"Mother!" I almost shouted.

She took my arm. "Go and catch the Goodies, love. If they get past Sergio's we'll never get another free meal."

"Are you all right?"

And then the aging woman had gone and Mother was back. "Of course I'm all right. A little too much *vino,* maybe. But if you quote me to Cotton or Peter I'll deny the whole thing."

So I ran ahead and caught the Goodie Pack, still busy flagellating Mrs. Kansas or Iowa.

"Mrs. Smith okay?" one of them asked me.

"It's the heat," another Goodie said with conviction. "We should have stayed in Switzerland."

"Rubbish! Too much bustle. Too many museums!" That was another, definitely English.

Mother was full of interesting tidbits over lunch, and it distracted the tourists from noticing that they were having nothing but spaghetti for the third day running. But once the Pack had dispersed to its respective hotels and *pensioni* for the afternoon siesta, she seemed to run down. Then she surprised me by saying, "Meg, I want you to take the car to Civitella and get all the stuff Sylvia promised us we could have. Peter wants that typewriter and we need some more wine."

I said meanly, "Isn't one attack of The Blight enough?"

"That'll be enough impertinence out of you, Miss. Please do as I say."

Whenever Mother had said that kind of thing before I'd always known she was joking. That day I wasn't sure. "I guess you've forgotten. I don't have a driving license yet."

"You drive better than I do, as both you and Cotton never fail to point out."

"But what if some *carabiniere* stops me?"

"He won't. You're too big. You look at least eighteen. Put your hair up."

I was still at the age where to look older was a secret delight. And because I was tall and more or less filled out—though I often felt it was rather less than more—I was often taken for older than my nearly sixteen years, especially when I put my hair up in a twist at the back. I opened my handbag and took out a small mirror and propped it against the sugar bowl. As I pushed my hair up on either side and groped in the bag for hairpins I looked critically at my image. My nose is well shaped but too big. My mouth ditto. My hair is black and my eyes are a light gray. With my hair up I practiced what Cotton calls my Gioconda Smile.

"It's more effective when you don't smirk," Mother said brutally.

"What's the matter, Mom? You sound cross."

"Nothing's the matter. I'm going to spend the next three hours at Maria's, taking a long nap. So don't rush back from Sylvia's. Why don't you take a swim in the lake? Anyway, no need to hurry. Maria'll be on the point of taking her nap when I arrive there, and she doesn't like to stir before four. I'll meet you at the Duomo at four fifteen." And with that, Mother slung her straw handbag strap over her shoulder and stalked towards the big and rather hideous cathedral, called the Duomo, and past that to the little piazza on which Maria had her attractive apartment.

"More *caffè?*" Sergio asked, coming up with a dust cloth in his hand and most obviously wanting to shut up shop for an hour or two himself.

"No thanks, Sergio. *Ciao.*" And I went out and down the street to where we had parked our car.

Civitella's full name, though no one ever used it, was Castello di Civitella di San Andrea, which meant "castle of the community of St. Andrew." It belonged to the Conte di San Andrea, an impoverished young man who was only too glad to rent it each summer to his Anglo-American cousin, Sylvia Matthews. She took it for four months and invited all her friends on several continents to come and see her. Along with everybody else, I loved going there. It was informal; the people there came in all varieties of nationality and age and sex, and there were usually, particularly in August, some young people staying, camping in sleeping bags up in one of the huge empty rooms at the top of the castle or out in tents on the grounds. And there was always swimming.

Although Sylvia was a lot older than Mother, they'd been friends as long as I could remember. The wine we drank at the cottage came from the farms around the castle, and this summer some guest had left an ancient portable typewriter at which Peter had cast lustful eyes. It was much

18

easier, he claimed, to write pornography by typewriter than by hand, whereas canon law, being a noble occupation, came more easily in the ancient way—by pen. Sylvia then said she could hunt up an old quill pen if he thought it would be even better than a ball-point. But Peter, whose sense of humor evaporated on anything concerned with canon law, said huffily that that would not be necessary.

No *carabiniere* stopped me. (I hadn't thought one would!) So I pushed our wheezy Fiat up the unpaved, bumpy path that led from the road direct to the castle. The first glimpse of Civitella is quite a sight. On top of a hill, its gray stone, rising above tiers of trees, looks almost pink in the soft Umbrian light, especially at either early morning or late evening. But even at two o'clock, at which ungodly hour I arrived, with the sun baking down on its crenelated towers and the tawny fields below, it still had a pinkish gold glow.

Narrowly avoiding a flock of geese that were quacking and honking as they bustled importantly down the middle of the path, I swept around a hairpin curve slanting up at a forty-five-degree incline, through the main stone arch, managed to avoid the statue of the armored figure that Sylvia referred to as The Ancestor, went around the castle itself and under another arch into a courtyard.

The courtyard was square. On one side, built into the wall of the castle compound, was the house occupied by the *fattore,* or agent, who managed the estate, and his family. Opposite reared the castle, the entrance up some steps to enormous double doors, now wide open. The other two sides contained arches, under one of which I had just entered. Between that entrance and the agent's house was the chapel with its bell tower or *campanile* rising above the great walls. Six cars were parked in the courtyard. I recognized the Volks owned by the agent. Then there was Sylvia's German station wagon, bought largely to aid in the transportation of whole families of children; an English Bentley with right-hand drive; two more Volks and a Fiat. The Bentley told me there were English people visiting, but the Volks and Fiat could mean anything.

A hot silence filled the courtyard. Nothing stirred. Even Castle Cat, a scrawny adolescent tiger, was asleep in about four inches of shade next to a stone wall. The only moving creature was a chameleon running up the stone urn in the center of the courtyard and changing before my eyes to a delicate green, the color of the fern and green leaves growing out of the urn. The louvers of the windows in the agent's house were all closed. So were those of the castle rooms overlooking the courtyard. I had arrived in the depths of siesta time, so what else did I expect? And what else did Mother expect when she sent me here at this hour?

Feeling a slight sense of grievance, I decided to check the terrace, an elegant name for a rather sandy stretch of grass through the opposite archway. Going through, I saw the usual litter of wicker chairs, most of them unoccupied. Two, however, had occupants. Two pairs of feet were propped up on the low wall below which lay the road by which I had come and beyond that, the whole stretch of the Tiber valley. A hat was over one face and an open newspaper over the other. From beneath the newspaper came rhythmic snores. I lingered to see if the snores had an English, American or possibly French accent, and decided that their tempered regularity argued an English owner. But I was still no nearer to Sylvia. I went back through the archway, ran up the steps and entered the castle.

The one place where there might be signs of life was the sitting room, up another flight. So I ignored the banqueting halls—never used anyway, except as overflow floor space for the young with sleeping bags—and the bedrooms beyond, and went up another flight into the sitting room that overlooked the terrace.

It was a large, square, comfortably untidy room. There were jigsaw puzzles in the making on a table by the door and another beyond by the window. Through the window I saw the range of mountains that ringed this part of the valley. Sitting bolt upright in a wing chair, eyes closed, was Sylvia Matthews, her silver head unbowed. Scattered around were some open chocolate boxes.

"Have a chocolate," Sylvia said suddenly, without opening her eyes.

"Thanks. I will. Do you have enough to go around?" I eyed them hungrily.

"More than enough. Everyone seems to be on a diet. Take all you want."

I promptly removed the three most promising bonbons from the nearest box and started peeling the silver paper off the first.

Sylvia opened her large brown eyes. "Your mother

called and said you'd be here. I'll ask Ernesto to put the typewriter in your car."

"Isn't Ernesto having his siesta?"

"He can wake up early. Why don't you go for a swim for a while? All the young people are down at the lake."

"I don't have a bathing suit with me."

"You can look in that cupboard halfway down the stairs. You're bound to find something that fits you."

"All right. Thanks. Who's there?"

"The Chadwicks from Suffolk and my cousins from New York, the Martins."

I nibbled my third chocolate. "Anybody else?"

"Yes, Cousin Giselle and her boyfriend, Pierre. And Conrad Saracen."

"Okay."

Just as I was leaving the room, Sylvia, who had appeared to be going back to the game of patience spread out in front of her, said, "How's your mother?"

"Fine. Why?"

"Just wondered. Didn't have time to ask her on the phone."

I found a bikini that seemed the right size, took the car down to the bottom of the hill and parked it beside the little shrine sitting over a small trickle of water. From there I walked over the hill and down to the reservoir, changing into the bikini on the way when I hit some shrubbery.

For those who didn't mind the insects known as waterboatmen, the frogs, gooey reeds and even, occasionally, a water snake, the reservoir was a jewel in the center of

Eden. About a hundred and fifty yards across and two hundred long, it had been artificially made by the present count's uncle to increase the badly needed water supply for the thirty-odd farms surrounding the castle. Along with the frogs and the snakes, another minor disadvantage was the ankle-deep mud that rimmed the edge of the water. One of the guests of a previous summer, however, had dragged two big pipes down and made a rough and ready causeway into the water, and when another guest, a plump middle-aged writer with a poor sense of balance, had wobbled off the pipes into the mud and emerged black all over instead of simply from the ankles down, he had thoughtfully placed some wooden staves along the side as props.

As I crested the hill there was a shriek and a splash and several bodies fell off a rubber raft floating in midlake into the water. At first it looked and sounded as though there were about fifty young people, but a second count placed them at about ten. More middle-aged types were sitting on the bank on towels, under large straw or cotton hats, reading, doing crossword puzzles and uttering familiar admonitions to the very small fry playing with another raft near the water's edge.

"No, Robert, it's Betty's turn now, get off the lilo at once and let her have it!"

Muffled yells and lots of splashing ensued. "Robert, I told you, get off and let Betty have it!"

More yells, followed by a protesting treble squeak, "Mummy, he won't let me get on. He's being beastly!"

There was a sigh from under a particularly tattered

cotton hat. A crossword puzzle was put aside and a male back rose and started down to the water's edge.

"Robert!" it said quietly.

A small boy in scarlet trunks immediately abandoned the raft, and an even smaller girl in a blue one-piece bathing suit got on.

"That's a good boy," Mark Chadwick said and headed back towards his crossword puzzle.

I reflected that even without the English accent I would have known those were English children. If they had been American the argument would still have been going on and probably been added to by a dispute between husband and wife as to conflicting rights of expression.

Having always, wherever I was, except for brief visits to the States, been a foreigner, I have become an observer of national types. I said something like that once to an American teacher at the university, a friend of Cotton's, and was severely reprimanded and given a lecture on the general theme of "All mankind shall be as brothers 'neath thy tender wings and wide" (Schiller, "Ode to Joy," Beethoven's Ninth). I didn't argue back. For one thing it's no use. People will think what they want to think. For another, the next logical observation I might have made would have brought even more trouble: If you tell English or French people, even those young and liberated, that they are behaving according to national type—that is, they are being super-English or super-French—the chances are they'll be pleased. If you say that to an American, you'll have a fight on your hands. It's odd. Or at least, to a non-native American who's never lived there like me, it is.

Once, about a year before, I asked Mother about it. After all, she hadn't left what she referred to as Possumtrot, Alabama, until she was seventeen.

Mother said indignantly, "Are you *complaining*, Mops? I couldn't wait to get out of that place. I would have given my soul to have been brought up in places like this—" and she waved her arm around the piazza in Florence where we happened to be sitting at the moment.

"Was it that bad?" I felt a little defensive. The question of what the word "home" meant was one of the few areas in which Mother and I had problems of communication. To Mother it meant the States, whether the hated Possumtrot or New York City or San Francisco. To Peter it meant England. To me it didn't mean anywhere.

"Yes. It was. Everybody knowing what you're doing and telling you to stop. And having to go to church every Sunday." For a minute she brooded over the remembered indignity. "You should be *grateful*, Mopsy."

"What for?"

"For not having to put up with that."

I sucked on the straw stuck in my orangeade. Cotton said, "Being brought up a perpetual exile isn't all heaven, Phoebe. It has its problems, too. As one myself I know what Mops is talking about." Cotton's father was in the American Foreign Service and Cotton never even saw the States until he was about twenty.

Peter, who had been moodily gazing into his vermouth cassis, suddenly raised his head and declaimed in a loud, clear voice:

"In the name of the Empress of India, make way,
Oh Lords of the Jungle, wherever you roam.
The woods are astir at the close of the day—
We exiles are waiting for letters from Home.
Let the robber retreat—let the tiger turn tail—
In the Name of the Empress, the Overland Mail!"

Somebody at a nearby table applauded. Somebody else said, "Up the Empah!" An American voice said, "Kipling in Florence? He's got to be kidding!" Another American voice said, "He's probably a racist!"

Peter turned towards the last, who was sitting quite near. "My illiterate colonial friend, you don't know what the bloody hell you're talking about. Come, Phoebe, let us leave this rabble!"

He rose, a little shakily, and started to take Mother's arm.

"But not before paying your bill," Cotton said, also rising and groping in his pocket for money.

Mother threw me a darkling look. "Sometimes, Meg, you puzzle me."

Sometimes I puzzled myself, and I wasn't quite sure what I meant or why I got cranky on the general subject of "home." But there it was.

Cotton put his hand on my shoulder. "Would you like some more ice cream, Mops?"

"That's fattening," Mother said. "She's already had three."

"You only say that because you wanted three too," Cotton pointed out.

"Of course. It's not fair. Anyway, Meg might as well get in the way early of watching her diet."

"Why?" I asked indignantly.

"Because, as I said, you might as well get into good habits early. Although of course your father—" She stopped.

I always pounced on any details about my father. "What about my father?"

"Nothing important," Mother said airily.

"Come on, Phoebe, you can't leave the child there," Cotton said.

"Well, all I was going to say was that if Meg is as like her father as she's growing to be, then she probably won't have to worry about her diet—just her soul."

I ignored the spiritual aspersions and went straight for what was important. "Father was thin like me?"

"Long and dark and thin like you." Then she gave me the smile that had been known to melt hardened criminals for miles around. "But not as nice as you."

I was still thinking about this scene when Mark Chadwick looked up. "Hello, Meg. Sylvia said you might be down. How are you?"

His wife looked up and smiled. "Want a raft? Robert and Betty have had it for half an hour."

"No, thanks."

I liked the Chadwicks and stayed talking to them for a few minutes. Sylvia's guests only knew one another through Sylvia and usually only met once a year, yet it was exactly as though one had finished the last exchange with them five minutes before and were taking up from there.

After talking to them I ran to the section of the bank where I knew there was slightly deeper water and dived in, thus avoiding the mud. Then I struck out across the lake. I crossed to the other bank and then swam back to the mob around and on the second and larger raft.

"Who are you?" said a pretty, fair-haired girl sitting at the edge of the raft.

"Meg Grant. Who are you?"

"Barbara Martin. Yes, Sylvia mentioned you. You're Phoebe Grant's daughter, aren't you?"

"Well, Phoebe Smith's. She's now married to Peter Smith."

"Gosh. Is that number four or five? Sylvia said your mother's had lots of husbands."

"Oh, I don't know. She hasn't had that many," I said, and duck-dived to avoid further controversy.

This time I emerged beside a boy with brown hair. He had nice blue eyes and a crooked nose. "Hello!" he said. "You must be Meg. Sylvia said to be on the lookout for you. Welcome and all that!"

That was much better. I grinned. "What's your name?"

"James Buchannon."

"Hello, James."

"Would you like to join us in the battle line? We're about to make yet another assault on the raft. The Yanks, i.e. the Martins, have had it long enough. But, of course, you're American, aren't you? Perhaps you'd rather be with them." And he waved a wet hand towards the raft where Barbara Martin plus another girl and two boys were repelling would-be invaders who were shoving at them from the water.

"Oh, I think that kind of thing is silly. I'll be on your side."

"Good-oh! The plan is to dive and come up under the raft and push."

"Okay. Say when."

"When!" he yelled and turned bottom up. I took a gulp of air and followed and trailed his feet through the green rather muddy water. When we reached the raft he pointed up and we both swam upwards with all the force we could muster.

The next ten minutes were taken up with a water battle, amid shrieks and yells and splashings. Finally everybody swam over to the far bank and stretched out in the sun.

I lay there, and after a while a deep peace stole over me. There were occasional plops from the water as small frogs launched themselves from mud banks and reeds. The sun was heat on my skin and a huge whiteness on the other side of my eyelids.

"Do you go to school in Florence?" Molly Buchannon, James's sister, asked me.

"Sort of. Sometimes."

"Yes, but you must be ready for college, aren't you?" That was Barbara Martin. "I mean, you're about eighteen, aren't you?"

I thought about that before answering. My hair, though sopping wet, was still up. Instead of answering, I asked, "How old are you?"

"Sixteen. Almost."

I thought about telling her that I was also sixteen, almost, but decided not to. "Where do you go to school?" I asked instead.

"A school in Connecticut. So does Sally." Sally was her sister.

Molly Buchannon said, "You're an American, aren't you?"

"Yes," I said.

Barbara rolled over and sat up. "Are you really? You don't seem a bit American."

Molly said, "But you've been brought up in Europe, haven't you?"

Barbara said, "Lucky, lucky you. How marvelous. Being brought up in civilized surroundings. I envy you."

I wondered who she was parroting. I sat up. "Does anybody have the time?" I knew that Barbara did because I had seen the large and complicated watch she had on even in the water.

She looked at it now. "It's ten after three."

"I must go."

"But you've only just arrived," James said. He grinned up at me.

"Where are Giselle and Pierre and Conrad? Sylvia said they were here too."

Molly, enough like her brother James to be a twin, waved her arm towards the far end of the lake. "Behold the lovers."

Sure enough, almost hidden by a huge willow tree, two brown, bikinied figures were lying side by side, hands clasped.

"Conrad?"

"Somewhere down at the other end."

I turned my head. A tanned figure lay up on the grass at the end opposite from Giselle and Pierre.

"It's nice," Barbara said. "Everybody can do his, her and its thing."

"Don't go," James said. "Why rush?"

"I have to meet Mother at the Duomo in Perugia at four fifteen."

"Well it's not going to take you an hour."

"No, but I think I'll take a bath first. 'Bye." And I dived into the water and swam across the lake.

When I got back Sylvia was winning her game of patience. I went to stare over her shoulder. "That's good."

"Not really. I cheated."

"Can I have a bath? I feel a bit sticky."

"Of course. Use the bathroom down the hall here. And you can help yourself to a towel from the cupboard on the other side. Use my talcum if you want to."

"Sylvia," I said. "You're half English and half American, aren't you?"

Sylvia dug a king from under a stack and clapped it on another pile of cards. "I am."

"But what are you really? I mean, what country are you a citizen of?"

"Well, according to the English, who are very secure and therefore liberal about such things, I have dual nationality. According to the Americans, who are strict about citizenship, I am an American. I travel on an American passport. Why?"

"Because the English are always saying to me, 'You're an American, aren't you?' And the Americans always say, 'But you're not really American, lucky lucky you!' Why do they always run their country down?"

"Insecurity. And anyway, it's the fashion. The last residue of the colonial inferiority complex. The other extreme is fanatic flag-waving. They're both irritating. Are you having *angst*, dear?"

I started to say no and then found myself saying, "Yes. It's bewildering. Mother seems to think that the greatest blessing she could bestow on me was not to bring me up in Possumtrot, Alabama, wherever that is."

"And you sometimes feel that you're from nowhere."

"Yes. And when people talk about *home*, even though they may hate it, they mean somewhere in particular."

"But it doesn't mean anywhere in particular to you?"

"No."

Sylvia dug a queen, another king and two jacks from under the remaining stack of cards. "What time do you have to meet your mother?"

"Four fifteen at the Duomo. We still have to take the Goodies around the Underground City. I wonder if they'll ask if it's original?" And I told her about Mrs. Iowa.

It was after I had had my bath and two or three more chocolates that Sylvia dropped her bombshell.

"By the way," she said, as I picked up my handbag and was about to leave. "I've been debating whether or not to tell you something, but I've decided I will. Your father is coming to stay here next month."

2

      I turned around in the doorway and stared at her. "My *father?*"

"Yes. Your father."

It would be easier to understand how stunned I was if one also understood how unreal my father had always been to me. Alan Fraser Grant VI had always been sort of a bad joke between Mother and me. Of course, from time to time, I had asked questions.

"Mother, what does Father *do?*"

"You just don't understand about the Grants, Mops. They don't *do.* They *are.*"

"Jolly expensive, that," Peter murmured.

"Takes money, too," Cotton agreed.

"Grants always have money," Mother explained. "Grant *means* money in early Pictish." And she went off into her rippling laugh that made everyone around laugh with her. So that was added to all the other jokes about Father.

Another time, about two years ago during a picnic on Monte Subasio, above Assisi, I asked, "Mother, why did you and Father split up?"

Mother looked at me. She made her mouth prim. Her eyes got bigger. "You may find it hard to believe this, Mops, but it happened over a terrible mistake I made." She waited.

"What mistake?" I asked, with a certain amount of wariness, knowing that I was slipping into my role of straight man feeding her lines.

She sighed. "Well, there were two mistakes, actually. But they happened at the same event. I went to have lunch with the old . . . with your father's mother, Mrs. Alan Fraser Grant V. Mops, I don't want you to put this down in your memoirs, it's too shaming. I not only used the wrong fork, but later, at tea—horror of horrors—I picked up the cup from the table *without* its saucer. Do I have to tell you more? Those icy gray eyes of hers—all Grants have icy gray eyes, even those who don't start out as Grants, but marry them; they come with the wedding ceremony—*ANYWAY,* they fastened on my cup and so unnerved me that I dropped it. It was Crown Derby and broke into about

35

twenty-five pieces, and she kept telling me it was perfectly all right in the kind of voice that made me wish I were dead."

"My eyes aren't icy," I protested indignantly.

Mother leaned over and squeezed my hand. "No, darling, they're not. And you have me to thank for that. The moment I realized they were going to be Grant gray, I started sending warm thoughts in their direction and have been keeping up a steady flow ever since. One can't be too careful about such things."

I giggled, but said, "And you broke up with Father over that? What did it matter?"

"You don't understand, Mops. He failed to stand up for me before that horrible old woman. That's when I left, taking you with me."

"But I thought I wasn't born."

"You weren't. But you were on the way, so therefore obviously I took you with me. Don't make silly objections, dear. So tiresome!" And we all laughed again, although I felt, as I often do, that something was unfinished, or had been averted.

I remembered that picnic very well. The Goodies were back in their various hotels recharging their energies after having been marched up and down the nearly perpendicular streets of Assisi all morning. We had brought bread, cheese, fruit and wine and driven as close to the top of Subasio as the car would go. Then we left the car and climbed on foot to the huge rounded top. All around us to the far horizon, in shifting hues of blue and purple and green, lay the foothills of the Apennines. The sun was blistering, but we all had large hats and, anyway, we were so brown it didn't matter. On a hill near us some rather scraggly-looking sheep were nibbling at the short grass. On another were some horses. A skylark had just mounted into the blue.

Cotton, who had been sketching Mother with the charcoal and drawing paper he always lugged with him in his knapsack, said, "It's no use, Mops. Your mother is not going to tell you anything she doesn't want to."

"There's nothing to tell," Mother said indignantly.

"Isn't there?" Cotton replied, drawing one of those long, flowing lines that always made his sketches so alive.

I crawled around and looked over his shoulder. There, from the drawing, sprang not only Mother's likeness but her essential quality. I hunted around in my mind for the right word to describe it, but couldn't find it.

"No, there is not," Mother said.

Naturally, I knew there was. "What is it that Mother isn't going to tell me?" I asked Cotton a while later, taking his hand as we walked down the hill to where the car was parked. Mother and Peter were ahead.

"Nothing."

"Yes, there is, or you wouldn't have said 'Isn't there?' in that funny voice."

"I was just needling her a little. Don't take me literally, Mops."

"But Cotton—"

"That's enough. Don't turn into a nag." And he pulled his hand from mine and started running down the slope.

From having been only avidly curious, I became unhappy. Having Cotton mad at me was the worst thing that could happen. I ran to catch up with him. "I'm sorry, Cotton. I won't be a nag. I promise."

He stared at me for a minute. Then he pushed my hat back off my face and kissed me. That's why I will never forget that picnic. I was fourteen and I knew at that moment what bliss was.

But there was a funny aftermath. I was standing there with the lights dazzling and larks soaring and the whole universe in a state of ecstasy when I finally noticed that Cotton was looking less than ecstatic. In fact, he looked bothered. "What's the matter, Cotton?"

"Nothing. That is, well, at fourteen you're supposed to be a child."

"I am *not* a child," I said indignantly.

"No, you're not. My mistake."

"What do you mean, mistake?" But I wasn't really paying attention. Something within me was about to burst forth, and it did. "Cotton," I blurted out, "will you marry me?" Quickly, before he could laugh, I said, "In five years?"

"In five years, Mops, I will be thirty-two. I will probably have a wife and six children." He jumped down from the grass bank onto the road and I followed him.

"You won't have time," I said indignantly. "All right then, two years."

Cotton jackknifed himself into the back of the car. "I'm not going to spend my honeymoon in jail for interfering with the morals of a minor."

I crawled in beside him. "That's nonsense. Juliet was thirteen. So was the Virgin Mary. Isn't that right, Peter?" Everybody was always surprised to learn that Peter had been brought up a devout Catholic and still considered himself so, even though, as he put it, there had arisen between him and Holy Mother Church a few trifling problems, such as divorce.

"The Blessed Virgin," Peter said, putting the car in gear, "according to tradition, was fifteen."

"You see," I said to Cotton.

"This is so sudden," Cotton said. "You'll have to give me time."

Cotton was still taking his time, even though I had brought the matter up once or twice and was now nearly sixteen. But the whole thing had driven out of my head whatever it was that Cotton was hinting Mother wasn't telling me. Until this moment, standing in Sylvia's sitting room and learning that my father—that mythical monster—was actually going to appear in the flesh, I hadn't thought of it.

"There's something about Father Mother hasn't told me."

"There's probably a lot," Sylvia said, shuffling the cards. "I love and esteem your mother, but there's no getting around it, her reporting is on the imaginative and inventive side. When something doesn't fit, she leaves it out."

"What is it she's left out about Father?" Suddenly it seemed very important that I should know.

"My dear, I have no idea." She looked at me over the cards. "Tell your mother that I told you about his coming, won't you?"

"Did Mother know he was coming?"

Sylvia laid out two rows of cards before she answered. "You know, I think you should ask her that question."

As she spoke, suddenly the chapel bell started to ring, a deep regular toll. I listened for a minute, then asked, "Who died?"

"Old Pietro, Renata's father. She sometimes helps Lucia in the kitchen. Everybody's been expecting it for years. Don Ludovico was here early this morning." Don Ludovico was the priest.

"Who's ringing?"

"Lucia." Lucia was Sylvia's cook and wife to Ernesto, general factotum around the castle.

We listened in silence to the bell. "It's nice," I said, "ringing the bell when somebody dies. Like a public announcement—he was here, but now he's gone."

Surprisingly, at least to me, Sylvia said, "The Lord gave, and the Lord hath taken away. Blessed be the name of the Lord."

"That sounds like a quotation."

"It is. The Book of Job."

"I've never read Job."

"You should. It's enlightening. It says something important about something important."

"Which is?"

Again she astonished me. "The relationship between God and man."

"Do you believe in God, Sylvia?"

"Of course."

"I don't know anything about God."

"I shouldn't worry too much. He knows about you."

We listened again to the toll, steady as a pulse. Then Sylvia said, "Ringing the bell is a kind of mourning. I sometimes think people have forgotten how to mourn." She looked up and gave me the warm smile that is surprising on her somewhat austere face. "Come here, child, and give me a kiss before you go."

I went over willingly enough. Next to Mother and Cotton I've always liked Sylvia best of anyone. There is something very rocklike about her. I sometimes have this fantasy that if the world came to an end, with tidal waves rising all around and Visigoths rushing in in skins and pointed teeth, she would sit there playing patience and somehow making them all ashamed of themselves.

"My dear," she said. "You are a good girl and by that I mean you have a warm heart and intelligence and common sense. And the greatest of these, I sometimes think, is common sense. But even though you are older than you should be, you are younger than you and your mother think you are. If ever you need me, at any time, and no matter what, I shall be here. Remember that."

Even though I wasn't quite sure what she was talking about, it was comforting. I leaned down and hugged her. "I will."

I watched her play for a minute.

"You're going to be late meeting your mother," she said.

"Yes, I know. But if I'm not there she'll simply meet the Goodies at the entrance to the Underground City and I'll find them all there. Sylvia, I never even knew you knew my father. I didn't know *anyone* knew him, though I suppose that sounds silly. How long have you known him?"

"Practically all his life. He was four years old when I first met him. His mother is a remote cousin."

I couldn't believe that all the time I had known Sylvia, she had known my father. "But why didn't you tell me you knew him?"

"I suppose I could make the obvious and silly reply that it was because you didn't ask. But that's not it. Given the separation and the divorce I saw no purpose in bringing up the subject."

I stared at her for a minute. "What's he like? Mother says he's stuffy and that the Grants think they're the kings of the earth."

The brown eyes looked up at me. "I think I'm going to let you answer that question for yourself when you meet him. Now run along. You're a great help to your mother with all those silly tourists and she'll need you more and more."

"What do you mean?"

"I mean none of us is getting any younger. Now do as I tell you and run along. I'm tired and I haven't had my nap and I have Ernesto to worry about."

"Why, what's the matter with him?"

"He's succumbed to another fit of lechery and has been making advances to one of the guests. It's most awkward, because his wife is such a marvelous cook."

"Why don't you tell her and let her take care of it?"

"Because she's twice his size and would kill him and then where would I be? Go away, Meg. I must sleep and think."

I knew she was getting rid of me and I only half believed her tale about Ernesto. He was inclined to be a pincher, but I suspected Sylvia told me that just to get me off the subject of Mother and Father.

By exceeding the speed limit in the best Italian tradition, with the typewriter and bottles of wine rattling in the back of the car, I arrived at the Duomo only five minutes late. Mother was not there, but Maria, her friend, was. Maria is half Italian and half English. She's a scholar of fifteenth-century Florentine poetry and is always being called in when manuscripts turn up and need verifying and putting into modern Italian. In appearance she is all Italian, with the dark gold hair and slate blue eyes of the *quattrocento* madonnas. In sound, she speaks almost unaccented English English.

"Look, Meg, can you take the Goodie Pack around the Underground City? Your mother's not feeling too well and I persuaded her to stay horizontal for a bit."

I realized then that I had been getting warning signals all day. There was Mother's funny look at the museum, Sylvia's cryptic statement, and her asking when I first arrived, "How's your mother?" and sounding as though she meant it and was not just being polite. Something seemed to squeeze my inside. "What's the matter with her, Maria? I thought she'd just drunk too much wine. But it's more than that, isn't it?"

"Yes. I'm afraid so."

"Well, what is it?"

"They don't really know. She's going to have to go to the hospital for tests."

"What do you mean, 'they'? Has she seen a doctor?"

"Yes. That's where she was this afternoon."

Worry really clamped down on me. Mother had always loathed doctors and medicine and said, whenever she felt less than her usual ebullient self, that she preferred to have what she called Healing Thoughts. Since these were nearly always accompanied by an ice pack and aspirin, I never accorded them the spiritual significance that perhaps they deserved.

I'm afraid the Goodie Pack got short shrift that afternoon as I raced them through the Underground City. The Underground City, which is actually my favorite "sight" in Perugia, is a recently excavated area of that mediaeval city and is wholly intact. Sometime in the Middle

44

Ages the city-state of Perugia lost a skirmish in its endless war with the pope, at which point His Holiness, as punishment and to show who was boss, evacuated part of the city which rose, tier by tier, up a hill and built himself a palace on the roofs of the evacuated houses and streets. Several centuries and numberless skirmishes later the Perugians drove out the papal forces and blew up the palace. Not long after that, archaeologists discovered the old city beneath—streets, houses, halls, rooms, ovens—everything unaltered. Going through it was like turning a corner and walking into the fourteenth century.

When the tour was over and the tourists climbed into various conveyances to take them back to their hotels and *pensioni*, I drove back up to the top of the city and straight to Maria's apartment. To the left of the entrance I saw Cotton's ramshackle car and realized he and Peter must have driven over.

Where I entered, the apartment is at street level. But because the house is fastened to the side of a steep hill, like every other building in Perugia, the terrace beyond the sitting room is at least two stories above the next street. They were all sitting on the terrace when I got there, sipping tall drinks and staring into the twilight across the descending roofs and the valley beyond to another hill, barely visible, up which climbed Assisi.

"Mother, are you all right?" I asked.

"Hello, darling. Yes, much better. I'm not sure whether it's the drink or that nice doctor."

"But what's the matter with you?"

"Darling, what a foolish question. You know no medical man is going to commit himself. First he has to draw all the blood from your body and send it to laboratories on four continents. Then he attaches you to various wires and computers which will almost certainly give you electric shock, and then, when you've died from loss of blood and shock to the heart, he'll offer a tentative diagnosis."

As I said, Mother is not Medicine's greatest friend. Nevertheless, I knew she was stalling. "But he must have given you some idea."

There was a silence. Then she said in a flat voice, "He thinks it's some kind of growth."

The word "cancer," unspoken, was nevertheless there in our presence. Nobody said anything. Peter reached out and took Mother's hand. Cotton got up and strolled to the railing and stood looking out on the incredibly beautiful sight. I went over to stand beside him.

"Does she mean cancer, Cotton?"

"I'm afraid so."

Far down on the street below, there was laughter and some shouts and running steps. Somewhere some music was playing. Across the valley a few pinpricks of lights appeared.

I knew I hadn't taken it in, that the reality of the dreadful word hadn't hit me. I went back over to Mother and stood behind her and put my hand against her cheek. "You'll be all right," I said.

I couldn't imagine that under any circumstances she would be anything but all right.

Mother put up her hand over mine. "Of course I will, love."

Cotton and Peter had brought some clothes for Mother and me and we were to stay in Maria's apartment for the next few days until the doctor got his tests back and could see Mother again. The shock of what Mother said had driven out Sylvia's news about my father for a while, but that night after dinner I said to her, "Sylvia told me my father was coming to stay at the castle."

"Yes, dear. I know."

"You know? Well why didn't you say something to me about it?"

"Because I wasn't sure myself till Sylvia told me."

"But you knew she was inviting him?"

"Yes." Mother was sitting at the long dressing table brushing her short, tawny curls. "Mops, do me a favor?"

"Of course. What?"

"Let's not talk about it for the moment. I want you to meet him first and then we can talk about it."

I was furious, and if I had not been overwhelmingly aware of Mother's having this thing, would probably have lost my temper and told her so. But as I stared at her face in the mirror and she looked up and back into mine, I couldn't do it. When Mother is happy she's a *gamine*. When she's unhappy she's a waif, and she looked more waiflike than ever tonight. It occurred to me that she was thinner than she had been. She's petite, but since she's given to wearing tentlike dresses, I hadn't noticed. I could see now, though, that the bones of her face were more prominent. The softness had gone, and with it that absurd youthfulness.

I went over and put my arms around her neck and bent down and kissed her. And for the first time I was aware of fear, like a snake, inside me.

The tests confirmed everything the doctor had said and Mother went into the hospital for abdominal surgery. I had never been in a hospital before, and although I liked the looks of the nurses, who were Sisters of Charity and, with their winged hats, went by like schooners, I did not like the sense of illness and death that for me permeated the atmosphere.

It seemed to me the operation took forever. Peter, Cotton, Maria and I sat in the waiting room. The whole thing had happened so fast I couldn't believe that I was there while Mother was in another room being cut open.

In the three days before the tests came back and the doctor shot her off to the hospital, Mother had insisted on taking around one or two Goodie Packs that her friend at the travel agency had produced. We didn't have a bus and we couldn't do sightseeing in the grand manner. Mostly what we got were the odds and ends of those who had arrived without plan and suddenly decided they wanted to see something and were willing to arrange for their own transportation. And so I didn't have time to think or to talk to Mother and by the time evening came and we were back at Maria's Mother was too tired. "Not tonight, darling," she said on two successive evenings. "We'll talk about it tomorrow." But the next morning we were off and running to the museum or to Sant' Angelo's Church which was once a Roman temple or to the Underground City, or to do what Mother called Tiddle-de-poms, which were "sights" that could be visited and returned from quite easily in an hour or two: a single painting in a wayside church, or a monastery or a mountaintop village. Anyway, we never talked. Peter was no good with tourists and so he didn't go along, but he and Cotton hung around and all of us had dinner together each night.

The last night before the operation Peter stayed at Maria's with Mother and I slept on a sofa-bed in a small dressing room. I didn't know where Cotton slept. But in the middle of thinking about Mother's operation and Father's impending arrival I had time to think also that Cotton was supposed to have a girlfriend in Perugia, and to feel the talons of jealousy.

After we'd been in the waiting room about two hours I suddenly said to him, trying to sound casual, "Where did you stay last night?"

He looked down at me and ran his fingers around his short beard. "Now what kind of a question is that?"

I knew I had broken one of Mother's cardinal rules: Never be possessive. Nor could I imagine her ever jealous. I stared down at my toes and to my horror felt two tears slide down my cheeks. I hadn't cried since Mother had dropped

49

her bombshell about what she came to call her bulge. ("'Growth' is such an awful word, Mops. Like an aspidistra. I prefer to call it a bulge. After all, it does bulge somewhere.") I didn't know whether I was crying for Mother or about Cotton's spending the night with his girlfriend or what, but I wanted to be alone. I got up and walked to the far end of the waiting room and stared out the window. After a while I heard footsteps behind me. An arm went around my shoulders, and all of a sudden I was crying hard into Cotton's shirt front. He didn't say anything at all. He just held me, and some of the terror that had rushed through me like a black river seemed to recede.

After a while I borrowed Cotton's handkerchief and blew my nose. Then out of my mouth sprang words I didn't even know I had been thinking. "Is Mother going to die?"

"I don't really know, Mops. When the doctor comes out he'll tell us. I hope not. I hope everything's going to be fine."

I went back and sat beside Peter. His is not the kind of face that painters or photographers use when they want to show tragedy. His cheeks and his eyes are round and his nose is so short it's almost round, but just looking at him made me want to cry again. I remembered how he took Mother's hand and so I took his. After a bit he squeezed it and looked down and said, "Sometimes you're more like her than you know, Meg."

After what seemed like several more hours the doctor came into the room. He was a nice youngish Italian who had done graduate work at Harvard and his residency at the cancer hospital in New York.

He looked at Peter. "Mr. Smith?"

Peter stood up. By this time I was clinging to him rather than the other way around. The doctor looked at me.

"I'm her daughter," I said. "Meg Grant."

The doctor nodded. "We got out all we could. I hope we got everything, but, to be honest, we can't be absolutely sure."

I said, "Then Mother may die?"

He looked at me. "All of us will die, Miss Grant, including your mother. But whether she will die sooner from this, or later from something else, I don't know. I'm sorry. I wish I could be more definite. But I can't. In any case, she's going to be feeling a lot better in the immediate future."

"When can we see her?"

"Come back this afternoon."

Peter had stood absolutely still, but I could feel his arm quivering. The doctor waited to see if we had any other questions, then gave a tentative smile and left. Peter and I sat down again. After a while I saw that big round tears were rolling down Peter's big round cheeks. I put my arm around him and wondered why I wasn't crying. After a while Peter got out an unspeakably filthy handkerchief and blew his nose.

"Would you like to go out and find some coffee?" Cotton said.

Peter shook his head. "No, I'll stay. You go."

"We'll stay, too," I said.

"No, go. I'd rather you would."

I knew then that he wanted to be alone. So Cotton and I went to a café near the hospital and ordered two *cappuccini,* and sat outside in silence and drank them.

After a while I said, "Sylvia said my father is coming to stay at the castle. She says she's known him since he was four years old. I can't think why no one has told me that she knew him, like any other real live person."

Cotton grunted. "Well, you've always been asking questions about him; now's your opportunity to get them answered."

"You don't sound a bit sympathetic," I said crossly.

"What's to be sympathetic about?"

"You seem to think that it's absolutely nothing to be meeting your father for the first time when you're practically sixteen."

"Well, I don't think it's a major tragedy, that's for sure. People whose fathers have died don't meet them at all. So you're ahead."

"I wish he had died," I said, and horrified myself and startled the waiter by bursting into tears.

What I wanted was for Cotton to come over beside me and put his arms around me as he had done in the hospital and I kept waiting for him to do so. But he didn't. All he said was, "Stop feeling sorry for yourself."

I took my hands away from my face. "That's a horrible thing to say to me, especially now."

"Why especially now?"

"Because Mother . . . Mother may . . . because of Mother."

"If I thought you were really crying over your mother I might be more sympathetic. But I don't think you are."

I was about to give rein to my indignation when I noticed that Cotton looked pretty washed out himself. In fact, he looked as white as spoiled milk. "I'm sorry, Cotton. You're unhappy too." Like Peter, I thought. And then words that weren't even in my mind a moment before fell out of my mouth. "You love her too, don't you, Cotton?"

Cotton was staring down at the dregs of his *cappuccino*. He didn't say anything.

"Don't you?" I asked again.

"It's impossible *not* to love your mother, Meg."

I didn't say anything, but the drawing that Cotton had made of Mother on Monte Subasio and had taped to the wall of his cottage slid across my mind. I knew what Cotton was talking about, because the thing, the quality, that made it impossible not to love Mother was in that drawing. I, too, loved Mother. The thought that Mother might not get well was a black hole, a terrible void, an emptiness that my mind was avoiding by circling round and round. Nevertheless, I wished like anything that Cotton had said it was impossible not to love *me*. And I knew that I was a selfish pig and felt worse than ever.

Mother delighted everyone by getting well with what the doctor called indecent speed. The first time I saw her,

53

the day of the operation, she looked terrible. Her freckles—
I never realized she had so many of them—stood out like
polka dots and for some fantastic reason her naturally curly
hair was as straight as a string.

The second day she looked a lot better. And the third
day I found her looking in a hand mirror.

"I'm going to sue the doctor," she said gloomily. "Look
at this!" And she held out a strand of limp straight hair. "He
must be some kind of sadist who takes his revenge on
women when they're helpless under the anesthetic. I shall
report him."

"To whom?" asked Cotton. He was lounging in the
cubicle's one comfortable chair making vague motions with
his charcoal onto the drawing pad open on his lap.

"To the Italian version of the AMA, to the—" She
caught sight of what Cotton was doing and raised herself on
one elbow. "Andrew MacKenzie, how DARE you make a
drawing of me like this! Meg, stop him at once!"

I went across and looked over his shoulder. It was true
that Cotton had drawn her almost without hair, but it was
an elfin face that looked up from the roughly sketched
pillow. "You don't have to worry, Mother. You look like
Camille, or whatever her name was in the opera—Margue-
rite Gautier. Wan but seductive."

Mother held out her arms. "Armand! Armand!" she
moaned artistically.

The doctor came in. "Armand who?"

"I'm playing Camille," Mother said, and gave a
theatrical cough.

The doctor pulled back the bedclothes and bent over her. "Don't do that. You'll pull out the stitches. Have you noticed what a fine embroiderer I am?"

"I'm not interested in your needlework," Mother said. "I want to know what you did to my hair."

"What do you mean?"

"It went into your alchemist's lair curly and came out straight. I'm going to sue you *and* the hospital."

The doctor put back the covers. "It was just a little extra I did for nothing. How can you be so ungrateful?"

"Wait until my lawyers arrive. You'll be sorry. When can I leave?"

"Not for at least another week."

"I shall probably be picked bald by then."

"No. That takes at least another ten days. We like to remove the hair strand by strand."

"Ha ha," Mother said rather bitterly.

I went out with the doctor. Peter was at Maria's coming to grips with a new porn novel. None of us had any insurance and the thought of the medical bills had had a galvanic effect upon him.

"Doctor," I said.

The doctor turned and I thought what a nice-looking man he was. He was stocky in build but had a thin face and curly black hair. "Is Mother going to be all right? I mean—I know what you said right after the operation, but—well, surely if there were anything wrong she wouldn't get well this *fast.*"

"I'm afraid I can't add or subtract anything from what I said before."

"But isn't her getting well so quickly a good sign?"

"Of course. A sign of her basic good health and resilience and ability to mend."

"Well?"

He put a hand on my shoulder. "Take all the good signs as good and hope for the best."

"There's something you're not telling me. You're holding something back."

"I am holding nothing back. I am telling the truth and the whole truth because I believe that is best. Your mother is a very remarkable woman. I hope, I truly hope, that she will have no more of this trouble. But I cannot guarantee it. That is all I can say."

"All right. Thanks." He tightened his grip on my shoulder, smiled, let go and went down the corridor.

Mother came home six days later having worn down everyone in the hospital, even the redoubtable nuns. That is, she came back to Maria's, and she and Peter occupied the guest room. The convertible sofa in Maria's dressing room became permanently mine, and Cotton reoccupied the apartment he lived in during the winter and had hoped to rent out. Perhaps luckily, he hadn't found a tenant. The plan was to move back to the cottage in about another two weeks.

Money, never very plentiful among The Pride, had reached an all-time low.

"Something has to be done," Mother said dramatically, from Maria's chaise longue.

Cotton, who was, as usual, doodling on his drawing pad, said, "I got a commission in the mail from New York this morning, forwarded by my agent. Some new church in Westchester wants a modern madonna. I'd pay you a model's fee, Phoebe, if I had any cash."

"Why don't you do Meg?" Mother said.

"She's not the right type."

There flashed into my mind Barbara Martin's careless statement: "Sylvia said your mother has had lots of husbands." That memory was followed now by my own P.S. *Not exactly a virgin.* I felt so ashamed of myself for that that I went over and kissed Mother on the cheek. "I'll go and look for some Goodies," I said as expiation. I hated Goodies and I hated taking them around, but money was money, and we needed it.

Mother put her arm up around me and her face against mine. A huge tenderness filled me and a strange, terrible sadness, but I couldn't find anything to say.

"Why don't you go with her, Peter?" Mother said.

Peter was in a corner of the sitting room where he had put the typewriter I had brought from Sylvia's on one of Maria's card tables. "Can't," he said gloomily. "Have to get this done."

"How's it going?" Cotton asked.

Peter shook his head. "Can't seem to get it off the ground."

"How far have you got?"

"Chapter one, first line."

"Well," Mother said. "At least that's a start. What is the first line? Maybe we can give you a shove."

Peter took a deep breath and read in a loud, dogmatic voice, "They took off all their clothes."

There was a silence while we all thought. At least, I assumed the others were thinking how to get Peter on to the next line. I was thinking how super it would be if Cotton would help me with the Goodies.

"The trouble is," Cotton said, "you should have started further back and led up to it."

"What you need, darling," Mother explained, "is a slow seduction scene. Clothed, I think. They really have more clout that way."

Peter muttered to himself, tore the paper out of the typewriter and threw it on the floor. Then he rolled another one in and typed for a bit.

"That's it, darling," Mother said in a comforting sort of voice. "I always think a clean sheet of paper makes a fresh new start. Read us what you've just written—the new version."

Peter cleared his throat. "He helped her off with her coat."

"I didn't mean that far back," Cotton said, getting up. "Mops, I'll see you as far as the Duomo. I've got to go and wire my agent."

"You wouldn't like to take the Goodies around with me, would you?"

"No," Cotton said. "I would not. I'm behind with my

work and, anyway, I hate taking tourists around. I never know who are more stupid—those who ask questions or those who don't."

"You're a snob. What's wrong with being a tourist? Weren't you one when you first came?"

"I was a visitor. Don't you know MacKenzie's law? If they're bearable, they're visitors; if not, they're tourists."

We left the apartment and went out into the hot, still streets. It was about a quarter to four and everything was still closed, although farther down the Corso I could see one or two shopkeepers opening up. Just past the Duomo, Cotton turned towards the post office and I continued up the Corso in the direction of the two hotels where Mother and I knew some of the desk clerks. I was past the first when I heard someone loping up behind me. I turned and it was Cotton, his straight, coarse red hair looking damp and even more rumpled than usual.

"Changed my mind," was all he said. But my heart soared.

"Did you send your cablegram?"

"No. I can do that later. The trouble is, do you think I look respectable enough for Goodies?"

I examined him. His khaki shorts were frayed and had a hole in them. His shirt, also khaki, was not only sweaty, it was torn in various places. His long legs were bare and one of his sandals had lost a thong. As far as I was concerned, he was a thing of beauty and a joy forever and I was convinced that any female in her right mind would agree with me—a thought that did nothing for my peace of mind. But there was no getting around it: he exuded a sort of disreputableness. I was pondering this when I saw that there was a large streak of greenish paint somewhere in the general area of his stomach. I pointed to it with triumph. "I shall say you're a painter torn from your work to give expert opinions."

"Nobody'll believe you."

I took his arm. "Yes, they will. I'm very convincing."

We walked towards the hotel. "You know," Cotton said suddenly, "you shouldn't be doing this—making up neat little lies for tourists."

"What should I be doing?"

"You should be in school worrying about algebra and exams and boyfriends and rebelling against the establishment."

"What establishment?"

"That's the point. You don't have one to rebel against."

I took his arm. "I have you."

He didn't say anything.

We collected six rather tired-looking tourists who were willing to pay for two cars and ended up our tour with the church of Sant' Angelo, a round fifth-century church sporting a twelfth-century fresco portraying St. Agatha, the virgin saint and martyr, among whose afflictions was having her breasts torn off by her persecutors. I told St. Agatha's story, as much in Mother's colorful style as possible, while Cotton leaned against a nearby pillar, waiting for arty questions. The tourists gazed in silence at the fresco featuring the severed breasts on a platter. I waited for

60

someone to ask if the painting was an original. But I had underestimated the imagination of one elderly tourist. Pushing up her bifocals she stared at the plate and said in a matter-of-fact voice, "They look like poached eggs."

And, of course, they did.

There was a gasp and a giggle from others in the group, almost immediately drowned out by a shout of laughter from Cotton. The tourists left the church and piled back into the cars in a riotous mood, cheered even further by the thought that soon they would be able to put their feet up.

We tucked them back in their hotel and returned to Maria's apartment.

"How did it go?" Mother asked.

"Marvelously," I replied, and told her about the poached eggs.

"Oh dear. I don't think I'll be able to take any more tourists there without giggling. I almost wish you hadn't told me." She paused, and it was then I became aware of a tautness about her.

"What's the matter?" I asked.

She played with the fringe of the shawl covering her feet on the chaise longue. "Sylvia called. Your father is arriving on an eleven thirty train at Terontola tomorrow morning. Mark Chadwick is driving to pick him up and is coming by for you on the way. You and Mark will meet him."

A queer little shiver went through me. I glanced around. The others had all gone out onto the terrace.

Mother and I were alone in the sitting room. "You've never told me, Mother. Why is he coming now? Why hasn't he ever come to see me before?"

Mother raised her head and looked at me. Her face looked drawn, adult, tired. "Because he has never known until recently that you existed. I never told him." Her small, thin fingers played and worked with the fringe.

"What do you mean, you never told him? I always thought that when you walked out, pregnant, he was so angry and mean he never bothered to see me or support me or . . . or anything."

"Yes, darling. I know you thought that. I'm afraid I let you."

"But it's not true?"

"No. Not exactly."

"What do you mean by 'exactly'? Is it true at all? That he knew about me, but never bothered to see me, which is what I've always thought?"

Mother took a deep breath. "No, Meg. It's not true. I was pregnant when he and I—when we had our final quarrel and I left. But I was only about three months pregnant and had only just found out about it and hadn't told him."

"Why didn't you tell him?"

There was a long silence. Outside on the terrace I could hear Cotton's voice and then Maria's. Below that on the street someone must have been passing with a transistor because there was a burst of Italian followed by music. Inside the sitting room it was almost dark. I was standing in front of the chaise longue looking down at Mother, but I couldn't see her face.

"Why didn't you tell him?" I repeated, hearing my own voice, louder, harsher.

Mother gave a funny kind of gasp. Her slender, pretty hands went up to her face and I saw she was crying. Normally I would have been there, my arms around her, because she rarely cried and I couldn't bear to see it. But nothing was normal now. "Meg, darling. I didn't know . . . I couldn't be sure . . ."

"Sure about what? That you were pregnant?"

She dropped her hands. "No, darling," she said. "That you were Alan Grant's daughter. You see, when I ran away—I never told you this, but I ran away with Tony. And for a while we . . . we had been lovers. That was what the fight with your father was about. I'm sorry, darling. I'm sorry. I meant to tell you, truly. But I never could. I've always been too much of a coward to tell you."

3

Mark Chadwick arrived shortly after ten and we headed over the mountains to Terontola, which is on the main rail lines coming north from Rome and south from Milan and Florence.

"Where . . . where is Father coming from?" I asked, as we started up the huge hairpin bends that would take us to the top. It seemed funny to be talking about him in such a casual way, as though I had known him all along.

"Rome, I think. He arrived by air yesterday."

I had gone for a long walk after Mother had made her confession, but before I went I managed to ask her, through the anger that was beginning to choke me, how she could be sure, even now, that I was Alan Grant's daughter.

"Because you're exactly like him. There's absolutely no doubt. I've told you that before."

She had, of course. She was still crying and I was still standing there, too angry and upset to go and comfort her, when Peter came back from the terrace. He didn't say anything, just went over and put his hands on her shoulders. That was when I went for a walk to the other end of the Corso on the bluffs, then back and down side streets, then up again along the old city wall through the big Etruscan arch and to the piazza. Then I had a sandwich and went to a movie. When I got back everyone was in bed and when I drove off with Mark the next morning neither Peter nor Mother had left the bedroom, nor had Cotton shown up. So I was feeling abandoned, nervous, angry and sorry for myself.

I didn't feel like talking, and besides, I didn't know how much Mark might know, so we drove in silence up the mountains and down again onto the plains around Lake Trasimeno, where Hannibal and his elephants had defeated a Roman general more than two thousand years before.

I suddenly said to Mark, "I've never seen my father before."

"I know."

"Do you know why?"

"Not exactly. Is it important that I should?"

I don't know what made me say the next words. When I heard them coming out I was horrified. "Mother

65

wasn't sure he was my father. I could have been someone else's."

Mark didn't say anything for a bit. Below us the lake shimmered blue, reflecting the sky. On either side of the road the hills were covered with scrub and the beautiful waving yellow broom plant. Then Mark said in his clear English voice, "I like and admire your mother very much, Meg."

"Yes," I whispered, hating myself, but determined not to cry. "So do I."

He turned and smiled at me. "I know it's hard for you, but try not to be judge and jury. It doesn't achieve anything." Then he gave me his handkerchief.

We got to Terontola about twenty minutes before the train was due. Ten minutes later there was a flurried announcement over the loudspeaker that the train would be half an hour late.

"What was that all about?" asked Mark, who doesn't speak much Italian.

I told him.

"Let's go and have some coffee."

We went to a small espresso bar off the platform and each had two coffees. I went to the ladies' room. Mark browsed around the newsstand where he found a *London Times* only a week old, which he bought and started to read. Two trains came into the station from opposite directions with a whoosh and a clanging of bells. I started to feel sick. Mark folded his paper.

"There's a café across the piazza from the station. I'm

going over there. There's no rush about getting back. I bought a book and will be quite happy there whenever you and Mr. Grant are ready to go back to Civitella." And he strolled out of the station coffee shop and back through the waiting rooms.

I went out onto the platform and, in violation of all the rules posted in four languages, crossed the tracks to the far platform where I knew the Rome express would be coming in. I still felt sick and was sorry now I had drunk two coffees. I was terribly afraid the train would be late. I was also longing for it to be late. But far to the south, where the tracks joined, the round silver front of the train became visible exactly when the stationmaster had said it would. Finally, with enormous impact, like a cannonade of thunder, it roared into the station, slowed and stopped.

Doors flew open. People poured out. Those waiting gave shrieks of joy and welcome. Arms were flung around necks. There were loud kisses. To my right and left people hovered in clumps. I saw no one who could be remotely described as a long, dark, thin American. Finally the train spat out some steam, gave a shriek and a "thunk" and started to move. All at once people made for the underpass which was the legal way to get back to the station platform. Finally there was no one left except a couple of porters, two fat women, three small children and a figure, far to my right—a tall, thin figure coming towards me.

I stayed where I was. My heart was pounding in a crazy, jerky way, and I was staring into the sun. Finally he came out of the sun under the roof above the platform and

moved towards me. He stopped a few feet away. I saw a
pair of gray eyes and a thin bony head like mine covered in
black hair flecked here and there with gray.

"You must be Meg," he said.

"Yes. I'm Meg."

He didn't move for a minute. Then he came up and
put his hand out. I took it and we shook hands formally.

"We go this way," I said, deciding in favor of the
lawful approach, and plunged down the underpass.

When we had emerged on the other side he said,
"Sylvia said there was a bank near here where I could get
some traveler's checks cashed. I'm afraid I didn't have time
in Rome."

"Yes. Just across the piazza. I'll show you."

Terontola is about the size of a polka dot, so we were
there in a minute. Out of the corner of my eye I could see
Mark, his dilapidated straw hat tipped over his face, reading
away at a thick book.

"Here," I said.

My father looked up at the name over the bank. "My
Italian is poor, but surely I'm not seeing what I think I'm
seeing."

The tight feeling in my stomach eased just a little. I
grinned. "That's it. Banco di Santo Spirito. The Bank of the
Holy Ghost."

He laughed, and it was like looking at my own face
laughing. "Will you come in with me or would you rather
wait outside?"

"I'll wait here."

So I stood outside the Bank of the Holy Ghost and waited for my father and wondered why I didn't feel anything at all.

As I waited for Father to come out, the almost certain prospect of long agonized silences punctuated by rushes of conversation seemed so dismal that I longed for Mark's calm good sense as a sort of buffer between us. Running the few feet to the corner of the piazza, I called Mark's name. He looked up. I waved and beckoned. He closed the book, rose, dropped some coins on the table and came loping across.

"Everything all right?" he asked when he reached me.

"I don't know. He's . . . he's inside cashing some traveler's checks."

Mark put his arm around me. "An entirely normal occupation. We'll just prop up the wall here till he comes out."

When Father emerged I introduced them, watching Father's face. "This is Mark Chadwick. He drove me here and will drive you . . . us . . . to Civitella." Was that subtle change in Father's features relief or disappointment?

The two men shook hands and we strolled back to where the car was parked outside the station. I went ahead and got in the back seat. When the two men reached the car Mark and I spoke at once.

Mark said, "Mr. Grant, would you like to sit in the back seat with Meg?"

I said, "You *must* sit in front where you can really get a view of the mountains as we go over."

Father hesitated, then got in the front seat with Mark.

I've read a lot about the insincerities of polite conversation and how unreal and ungutsy it is. Civil inanities, Peter calls it, and Mother and Cotton don't have much time for it either. But Mark, who can be both direct and honest, can also, in his own words, waffle on endlessly. It is, he claims, his greatest talent, and he certainly exerted it in that drive back over the mountains, while I sat in the back almost paralyzed with anxiety and gratitude. Every now and then he'd pause to see if either of his companions had become unfrozen or if the atmosphere had loosened up. But when it started getting electric again, off he'd go, asking Father about the weather in New York, talking about the weather in London, the roads in Italy, the congestion at the Rome airport, and every now and then Father would join in with the congestion at Kennedy Airport, the awfulness of New York in summer and how easy it was to lose baggage, and so on and so forth.

An hour later, having also touched lightly on the Umbrian school of painting, the bad olive and wine crop of the previous year, the oil embargo and the necessity of having one's car lubricated every so many miles (to none of which I contributed although both Mark and Father periodically tried to draw me into the conversation), we arrived at Civitella.

Mark and Father went on upstairs into the castle. I went out onto the terrace and sat down on the wall. A late lunch, I knew, must be awaiting the three of us in the dining room, but I couldn't move, and, anyway, I wasn't hungry.

I don't know how long I sat there staring at my toes and at a scorpion that waddled back and forth along the ground, tail aloft. After a while I heard feet on the stones of the courtyard and my father appeared in the archway and came across. He was still wearing his light gray sports jacket, dark trousers and red tie with white polka dots. His nose, I noticed, tilted a little at the end, like mine. He came and sat down on the wall beside me. After a minute he said, "That would appear to be a scorpion."

"Yes. There're quite a lot of them around."

"I take it they're not lethal."

"No. Although they can give you a nasty sting."

"I remember them from army maneuvers in Texas. They used to come into the tents and get in sleeping gear."

"I didn't know you were in the army," I said. Then, after a longish pause, "I don't know anything about you at all. And you don't know anything about me, do you?"

"No. Not yet. But I came so that we . . . we could get to know one another."

What Mother had said about not being sure whose daughter I was kept coming back, like onions after a meal. "Did you have any doubt about . . . I mean, whether I was . . . ?" I saw then how the sentence would sound, and I didn't want to be disloyal to Mother, especially in front of Father.

"None at all. Your mother sent me a picture of you."

"Oh." It was then that the obvious question I had not asked Mother hit me. "I wonder why Mother wrote to you now, all of a sudden."

"I'm not sure." He paused. "Has she been all right?"

I turned and stared at him. "What do you mean, all right?"

"I mean, is she well?"

"Why? Why do you ask that?"

He straightened up and stood, and then put one foot on the low wall. "I'm not sure. I had a feeling from the letter that she wasn't, or thought she might not be."

"When did she write?"

"About two months ago."

I thought. It had been barely three weeks since Mother had had her faint spell at the museum, and it was after that that she had gone to the doctor and then to the hospital. Unless, of course, this had happened before and I hadn't known it. My heart gave an odd thump. I stood up. "Three weeks ago a doctor told Mother she had a growth—cancer. She went to the hospital immediately and had it out and is now back in Maria's apartment. I thought that that was the first warning she'd had . . ."

"But you think she might have known before and written to me on that account?"

"What did she say?"

"Just that you existed, see photo, and that for a lot of reasons that now didn't seem as important as they once had, she hadn't told me, but that she thought now I should know, in case anything should happen."

"In case anything should happen?"

"Those were her words."

I felt baffled and helpless, and since I'm not used to feeling either, it made me feel cross. "You didn't exactly rush over, did you?"

"I came as quickly as I could. I have other obligations."

"I'm sorry. I didn't mean to be rude. I don't suppose you wanted an unknown daughter dumped down in your lap."

He said roughly, "Of course I wanted to know about you." He paused. "But that doesn't make the whole thing easy—for either of us."

"No."

There was another of those pauses. Then he took a breath and said lightly, "We have to begin somewhere. Why don't you tell me about yourself?"

I pulled a leaf from the branch of the huge tree above us. "What do you want to know?"

He made a gesture with his hand. "Where do you go to school?"

"Wherever we happen to be at the time. I mean—last winter it was a small English school in Florence, the year before that it was a school in Vienna. The year before that it was Florence again, and then in past years in Belgium, France, England, Spain . . . Switzerland." To myself I sounded like a travel agency.

"You must be something of a linguist."

"I suppose so."

"When you say 'we' do you mean you and your mother?"

73

"And Peter, Mother's husband, my stepfather. Also sometimes a friend of ours, Andrew MacKenzie. We call ourselves . . ." My voice trailed off.

"What do you call yourselves?"

"The Pride. It's sort of a joke." It didn't sound very funny.

"The Pride. . . . Yes, I see." It sounded polite, remote and unamused. Another pause. "I take it your stepfather was working in these various places. Sylvia wrote me he was English. Is he in the Foreign Office?"

A vision of Peter suddenly rose before my eyes, his scruffy shirt, bitten fingernails, eyes round like a child's. "No. . . . He's a writer . . . and a specialist in mediaeval canon law."

"I see, a scholar. Is that what he writes about—canon law and kindred subjects? Is that what he does for a living?"

I became quite sure that Father knew all about Peter's porn and that he was trying to pin me into a corner so that he could do something to Mother.

"Why do all Americans always ask about what people do for a living? Don't they ever think about anything but money?"

Father took his foot off the wall and bent down. "Here's a four-leaf clover. It's years since I found one." He straightened and sat down on the wall, his legs out in front of him. The four-leaf clover lay in the palm of his hand. He said, "Isn't that a bit sweeping, Meg? There are more than two hundred million Americans."

"All right. I'm sorry. But they do seem to ask that question. The ones I've met."

"And what do other people—the non-Americans—ask?"

As a matter of fact, I hadn't particularly noticed. I thought for a minute. Then I said, "Well, usually, what part of France or Italy or England or wherever does he or she come from?"

"So they identify with place, rather than with job."

"I suppose so. Americans seem to move around all the time."

"Well, in that, at least, you should be able to identify with your fellow countrymen. You've moved around a lot."

"I don't particularly want to identify with them."

The rude words, pushing him away, came out of my mouth almost without my volition.

"Meg, you are obviously angry at me and resentful of me. Is it because, as you put it, I didn't rush over as soon as I heard from your mother?"

I had no idea why I felt the way I did, so I said the first thing that came into my head. "You were mean to Mother. Everybody loves Mother except you, but you were mean to her. You drove her away." And the minute I said it, I knew that Father would know I could only have got that from Mother. Fear for Mother, and guilt, rose above my anger. "Sylvia told me," I said quickly. I was so afraid that he would demand details of how and when that I rattled on. "I can't call you Father. It doesn't feel right. So I don't know what to call you."

"Call me Alan, if you like."

The moment he said that I felt better. Everything inside me seemed to calm down. He seemed farther away and therefore safe to look at. I glanced at him then for the first time since he had sat down. He looked kind and tired, like any other middle-aged man.

We had another silence which, like the previous ones, would have started being uncomfortable except that Sylvia appeared in the archway and moved slowly towards us. She had on a cotton print dress and sandals. Her white hair was piled on top of her head. Around her shoulders was a paisley shawl. Dangling from her arm was something very like an old-fashioned reticule, which contained, I knew, at least one pack of miniature cards as well as all the letters of a Scrabble game. In her hand she was carrying a Scrabble board and a book of Double-Crostics. Behind her came Ernesto bearing a small tray.

"Hello dears. I thought I might join you. Just put the tray on the wall, Ernesto. And bring that table a bit nearer."

Ernesto put the tray down beside me and I saw that on it were a plate with sandwiches, two glasses, a small carafe of wine and a bottle of orange soda. Picking up a wicker table from the other side of the tree, he brought it over.

"You can bring coffee in about twenty minutes," Sylvia told him. "Now, dears," she went on comfortably as he left, "you haven't had any lunch. I think you'd both be the better for food. And I thought a game of Scrabble would be nice."

Having Sylvia there was a great relief. It was as though

her arrival had defused the bomb between us that might go off at any moment. Father and I (no matter what I had said about not calling him Father, I still thought of him as that, and would probably, in due course, get around to addressing him by that name) nibbled the sandwiches. He drank the light wine and I drank the orange. When Ernesto turned up with the coffee Father had some, but my stomach was still churning and I refused. All this while, Sylvia had laid out a game of patience on the table and was chatting away with Father while she played. I heard them without listening.

Turning a little, I stared out over the fields. Huge oaks shaded the terrace, their branches meeting, their leaves fluttering in the slight breeze. Beneath them it was shady and cool. But in the fields below and beyond the sun baked on the ripening wheat. The road we had come up, dried almost white by lack of rain, dipped down and then started to climb again up to the main road. There, where it met the road, marched a line of cypresses, tall and black in the afternoon sun. On the road itself a cart moved slowly, drawn by white oxen.

My father was also staring at the road. "That's a very biblical scene," he said.

"Yes." Sylvia swept up her cards and started to shuffle them. "I always think of Pharaoh and the kine."

"Kind?" I asked.

"No," Father said. "Kine. Oxen. Cattle."

"Oh." I didn't know what he was talking about, but I didn't want him to know that. "Would you like a game of Scrabble, Sylvia?"

"Lovely," Sylvia said. "Alan, you'll play, won't you?"

"No." He got up. "I think I'll go and unpack, if you'll excuse me."

"Of course. Why don't you have a bath?"

He smiled faintly. "Is it that bad?" The smile made him look a little younger.

"No. It's just that if you wait till before dinner, then you'll only get a trickle, if that. That's when everyone bathes, and our water pressure is not strong."

"A good idea." He smiled at me. "You'll be here for dinner, won't you?"

"No," I said. "I'm leaving quite soon. Cotton—Andrew is coming to get me at four."

"All right." He hesitated, then waved and moved off across the grass.

Sylvia said, "If you want Andrew to come and get you you'd better go and call him. Otherwise Mark will drive you back."

"How did you know that I hadn't already arranged it?"

"I just spoke to your mother on the telephone."

"I wish people would stop having conversations about me behind my back."

"Meg, dear," Sylvia said, taking out the Scrabble letters from her reticule, "you've never in your life behaved like a spoiled child, and I don't think you ought to begin now, even though I do realize that things aren't easy for you. But then, they aren't easy for any of us. Now then, let's each pick one and see who starts."

Accepting the rebuke, I picked an E. Sylvia picked an X. "You start, dear." She patted my hand.

"I'm sorry," I said.

"That's quite all right. I understand."

The funny thing was, I knew she did. As we played, the huge waves beating around inside me grew calmer. Sylvia is a ferocious Scrabble player, with a lynx's eye for making two, three and sometimes four words with only two new letters, and totting up enormous scores. It's very humiliating for me. I'm quite good at writing, but that doesn't seem to have anything to do with seeing how to make four words at once.

"That's eighty-one for me and thirty-six for you," Sylvia said complacently.

I stared at my letters. There were an N, an I, two Es, an A, a K and an O. Then I looked at the board. After a bit I built KINES on top of an S. "Kines," I said. "Cattle, like Fa— Alan used."

"I'm sorry, dear," Sylvia said, not sounding at all sorry. "But I can't allow that. 'Kine' is plural, like 'cattle.' You don't say 'cattles.' "

Muttering, I took the letters off.

"Try 'snake,' " Sylvia said helpfully.

"Thanks." I put the letters trailing down from the S. "It's all those Double-Crostics you do. I never heard of the word 'kine' before. Where does it appear?"

"In the Bible. Haven't you read about Pharaoh and his dream of the lean and the fat kine and Joseph and his coat of many colors?"

"No."

"Get your father to tell you."

"Why should he know?"

Sylvia stared at me over her half spectacles. "Well— it's more or less part of his profession."

I remembered, then, Father saying something about the scene being biblical. "You mean he's a biblical scholar?"

"In a way. Yes, I suppose he is. I mean, didn't he tell you? He's a priest. An Anglican priest."

"A *priest*," I burst out. "He's not dressed like one. He's not wearing a round collar."

"Well, dear," Sylvia said, gazing at the board, "he's not sewn into his vestments for the duration."

"Did you know my father was an Anglican priest?" I asked Mark, when he was driving me back.

"Yes. Sylvia said he was."

"I think somebody might have told me."

"Why? Do you find that alarming, something you should have been warned about? Would you have felt different if you had discovered that he was a doctor or lawyer or businessman or teacher?"

"Yes."

"Why? I know lots of priests. Most of them are quite human and unalarming."

"I always expect them to disapprove of things."

"Oh. Have the ones you've known been disapproving?"

I thought. "I haven't really known any, except Don Ludovico, who says Mass here on Sunday."

"Well, he doesn't strike me as particularly disapproving. Is he?"

"No. I don't know where I got it."

But of course I did. From Mother. Mother always held that ministers approved of nothing except going to church and not having fun. I suddenly remembered Mother saying one night at the cottage, "There was the Reverend Williams at home. He was absolutely *carnal* about the importance of denying oneself." And I started to laugh.

"Come along, now," Mark said. "Share."

So I told him, and he laughed too. "Still," he said, "I think your mother is a bit out of date with her prejudices. The clergy have loosened up considerably since being miserable was considered a lifetime dedication. Give him a chance, my dear."

"That's what everybody keeps saying."

"That means it's probably the last thing you want to do."

"Why do you say that?"

"Simple observation," Mark said with pride. "I'm a father myself."

"Did you know that Father was a clergyman?" I asked, bursting in on The Pride plus Maria, who were sitting out on the terrace of Maria's apartment.

"Of course, dear," Mother said with a little surprise. "You forget, I knew him."

81

"I wish I could meet him," Peter said.

"Why?" I asked. "Would you like to challenge him to a duel?"

"How old-fashioned you are," Peter said. "No, I should like to get his views on certain rather odd aspects of early twelfth-century canon law in its relationship to the state."

"He asked me what you did," I said ominously.

"Did he, now? Did you tell him about my novels?"

"No. I told him you were a twelfth-century scholar."

"I know I'm not very well preserved," Peter said, putting a hand on his paunch. "But I'm not that old. Perhaps you meant I'm a scholar of the twelfth century?"

"Why are you trying to make a grand opera out of all this?" Cotton asked.

Mother said, "Because she has been misled and deceived and is left with the task of trying to fit a clerical father into her life at a rather advanced age. Isn't that it, love?" And she held out her hand.

I went over and took her hand. "Mother," I said. "I love you very much."

"Yes, darling. I know you do. And I love you, too." And she reached up and gave me a big hug. I gave her one back. "You'll see, darling," Mother said. "Everything somehow will be all right."

And because she said it, it was true. But the somehow seemed rather far off and on the other side of a range of mountains that had to be got over in between.

4

Two days later, unwillingly, and only because Mother insisted, I packed up some clothes and went to spend a week with my father at Civitella. Sylvia had called the night before to suggest it. I had refused, and Mother had taken the phone from me and accepted.

"But I don't want to go," I almost yelled, when Mother had hung up.

I followed her back to the bedroom. Everyone else was on the terrace, but Mother had taken to going to bed soon after dinner. She was already in a filmy, sea green nightgown that made her look, I thought, like a painting I had seen of a sea nymph.

Mother sat down on the bed. "I know you don't want to go, darling, but I want you to."

"Why?"

"Because I think you should get to know your father."

"I don't want to get to know him. Besides—" The question that I had been afraid to ask rose up before me. "Why did you write to him two months ago, sending him a picture of me? Had you been to see the doctor before that day in the museum? Mother, are you all right? Is there something I don't know?"

Mother hesitated. Then she said, "Yes, Mops. I had been to see a doctor before. There was something—anyway, I went to a man in Florence."

"Why didn't you tell me?"

"I didn't think there was anything to tell. He talked in circles, not uttering a word of fewer than five syllables . . ." She paused. "I suppose the truth is, Mops, I didn't want to hear what he was vaguely hinting at, and anyway, you know how I feel about doctors. . . ."

"What was he hinting at?"

"He was hinting at what turned out to be true—that I had a tumor that should be operated on. Only it was so carefully worded that I could pretend it wasn't true. I guess I knew somewhere that it must be—because I wrote your father. Only that wasn't the reason I gave myself. I thought of it as an attack of conscience about not letting him know about you—letting you think that he did know but didn't care. . . . You know, Mops, I've never been very brave."

"That's not true," I said indignantly.

"In what way isn't it true?" Mother asked drily.

I didn't know in what way it wasn't true, or I couldn't think of any examples, so I said rather helplessly, "It just isn't."

She leaned over and hugged me. "You're a very loyal person, and I've always valued loyalty over tiresome virtues like accuracy . . ." She caught my eye. "And there's no need," she went on with spirit, "to give me that knowing look."

I grinned a little, recalling several graphic illustrations of Mother's preference for almost anything over accuracy. Then I said, "Mother, I don't want to go to Civitella for a week."

Mother didn't say anything for a minute. Then, "Please, Meg. Don't make me . . . make me plead with you. Pleading is worse than ordering. I can't tell you how much I've hated it all my life. Making people do things—'Do this because you love me,' or worse, 'because I love you.' That's why I ran away from home. I've never talked to you about Momma—I can't bear to remember it. The only way I could be free was to break her heart. That's why I couldn't go back. I never went back until she was nearly dead. She was in a home then. Had been for five years. And she didn't even know me. Everybody said it was senility. And it was, of course. But I used to think that she just disappeared inside herself, where my running away couldn't hurt her anymore. I went to see her finally. She was in a wheelchair. Had to be looked after like a baby. But still pretty, the way I remembered her. She was nearly blind by then, so they didn't bother with her glasses. I'd never realized how much her eyes were like mine, a sort of hazel green, and as clear as a child's.

"I stood in front of her and called her and tried to talk to her, but she didn't hear me or see me. Just stared past me, as though there were something else she could see. Meg, it was so weird. She wouldn't talk to me, didn't act as though she heard me at all. But I turned and spoke to Aunt Molly, who went with me. Aunt Molly was her sister, and Aunt Molly said something, a line of poetry that Momma used to read me, and Momma suddenly sat up in her wheelchair and finished the line. . . ." Mother was shaking and tears were running down her cheeks.

I ran over and put my arms around her and held her. "Mother, please don't. It's all right. I'll go. I promise."

"No, no, no, *no*," Mother said. "I don't want you to do it because I was crying. Don't you understand, darling? That's blackmail. That's why I ran away. That's even why I left your father, was unfaithful to him."

I felt my heart harden against Father. "You mean he tried to blackmail you?"

"No, darling. I didn't mean that. It's just that it happened so soon after I ran away from home. He was older than I was and fell terribly in love with me, and I with him . . . he was so good-looking, and so different from anything I'd known . . . but somewhere deep in me, I didn't believe I could be loved and be free . . . and I had to be free. And then I met Tony, and he was as wild as I was. . . . But I ran away from him, too. I've always run away, until I met Peter, and it's only been with Peter that I've been both free and loved, and that's why I love him so much. Everybody sees him as a sort of overweight clown, fiddling about with his Latin documents and his unsuccessful porn. But he knows how to love more than anybody I've ever known. And I'm not talking about sex, although he's good at that, too. But I don't think even in his mind he's ever tried to make anybody do anything. Probably that's why he's so unsuccessful . . . except in loving people. That's his real talent . . . loving."

I hugged Mother for a while and after a bit she stopped shaking and crying and I could feel her relax. Then I said, "Mother, whatever made Peter start writing porn? He's not very good at it, and I don't think he enjoys it."

Mother sighed. "No. He isn't. And doesn't. It all started as a joke with one of his mediaeval Latin tales. He was chortling away one night over some rude and bawdy student songs of the twelfth century . . . You see, people don't understand that in the twelfth century they didn't just sit around spouting theology and building cathedrals, although they did that, too. Peter says . . . what I mean is, for Peter there's no such thing as the past . . . it's all happening now." She paused. "It's very hard to explain."

"I understand. At least I think I do. Go on."

"Well. . . . Peter always says that everything—I mean the cathedral and the bawdy story were much more related then than they are now, only . . . Anyway, one night four or five years ago—we were in Paris then, and I was trying to find a job in one of the travel agencies and you were at the lycée—Peter was laughing at some long, randy tale in one of his mediaeval documents. So I asked him what it was about and he translated it for me, and we both laughed so hard that we got hiccups. Anyway, I said it would make a marvelous porn book—sort of like *Fanny Hill.* So he wrote the translation down in modern novel form and sent it off to a small, semiporn publisher who bought it immediately. We were tremendously set up and paid our bills for *weeks* almost on time. I remember because it was then that Peter said he thought it was almost bad for our characters to have our credit restored even for a while. It turned the mind in the direction of security. . . ."

Mother suddenly caught sight of my face, and reached up to pat it. "Yes, I know, Meg darling, you've always had a strong tendency towards things like paying bills on time. I can't think where you get it, except that my mother and your father had it. . . ." Her face clouded again. "I've spent all the years since Momma died not thinking about her, because it always hurt so much and made me feel so terrible, and now I think about her a lot. Anyway, that's how Peter got started writing porn, and as long as he just translated old Latin stories he did beautifully. But eventually they ran out and he had to start making them up and that's where everything went wrong, because you know, Mops, he just doesn't have that kind of a mind. He can spend *hours* over the smallest details of some twelfth-century monastery —who did what work, what kind of food they grew, how and when and where they prayed, their relationship to the community and the villages around them and so on—happy as a lark, but his mind really goes blank when he has to write an erotic scene. . . . In fact," Mother said with the air of making a confession, "I usually supply the details."

"In that case, I'm surprised they're not more successful."

"Yes, so was I. But Cotton says that mine aren't really any good either. He says that readers of porn are not interested in romantic touches, which are what I always find the best part."

The mention of Cotton depressed me. Mother turned her back to the head of the bed, putting pillows behind her. Then she looked at me and rubbed my cheek again "You love him—Cotton—very much, don't you, Mops?"

I nodded. "Yes. I once proposed to him, only I was younger then."

"What did he say?"

"Nothing," I replied bitterly. "He just joked around about tampering with the morals of a minor."

"Cotton's a bit like I've always been, Meg. He wants to be free more than he wants to love. There's no use trying to persuade him out of it. If you want him, darling, you must love him but leave him alone. I wish you were a bit older."

"Why? What's my being older got to do with anything? You mean because of Cotton? Do you think he'd love me more if I were older?"

"No, but I think he'd be less confused."

"Why is he confused?"

"Because he—or his reactions to you—can't figure out whether you're a child or an adult, and of course his confusion is perfectly right—you're not either one completely. You're a bit of both."

"Mother—" I burst out. "Do you think when I'm all grown up he'll be in love with me?"

"My darling child—" Mother leaned over and took both of my hands in hers. "How can I possibly tell? You mustn't ask questions like that! That's like . . . like trying to lock up the future, make it happen the way you wrote it. It doesn't work that way. You have to live a day at a time."

"That's the way you've always lived, isn't it?"

"Yes. It's the only way I could ever live."

"I'm not sure I can. Live like that, I mean. I don't think I'd be good at it."

"I know it won't be easy for you. Peter always said—"

"What?"

"That because you'd always been free, maybe you craved some sort of structure, the way I wanted freedom because I'd never been free. It's something like salt. If you don't have it you'll do almost anything to get it. Peter says tribal wars have been fought and people killed for salt. But too much is just as bad. You can die over that, too."

We didn't say anything for a minute. Then Mother said, "You will go to Civitella, won't you?"

"Yes, all right," I said. I didn't add, *Because you asked me,* because that would make her unhappy and make her think that she had maneuvered me into it, which was, of course, quite true. As I watched, Mother opened the drawer of the night table and got out a square white box. She opened the box and took out two capsules. I couldn't have been more amazed. I had never seen Mother take anything more than aspirin for hangovers.

"What are those?"

"Sleeping pills, darling."

"Can't you sleep?"

"No, darling, or I wouldn't be taking these, now would I? Bring me a glass of water from the bathroom, will you, Mops?"

I brought her the water and she swallowed the pills and snuggled down among the pillows. "Now I'm going to read until I feel sleepy. Somebody from Civitella will be coming to pick you up quite early in the morning, darling, so give me a big hug now."

I went and gave her a huge hug. She felt tiny. "Mother, am I growing again, or are you getting smaller?"

"You're growing, darling."

But it wasn't true. She was getting smaller. Under my arms and hands I could feel her ribs and the ridges of her vertebrae.

Not wanting to go and thinking about Mother's ribs and bones sticking out made me resentful of being at Civitella and of Father, so I took off in a rather sullen mood.

Mark, who had put someone on a seven thirty train in Terontola, called for me shortly after nine and drove me back. Then he dropped me in the courtyard and took the car and Lucia down to the local town to do some grocery shopping for Sylvia.

Ernesto took my bag and I followed him into the castle, up wide stone steps to the first floor, through a series of what used to be huge banqueting halls, the windows high in the walls, the ceilings fifteen and twenty and, in one case, forty feet up. Passing through the massive double doors to the central hall, whose ceiling rose to the battlements, we went into another hall and then turned left into a smaller room.

Prepared to repel all invaders, I waited to see if Ernesto was still suffering his attack of lechery. When he did nothing but put my bag on the luggage rack and say Signorina Matthews was upstairs in the dining room finishing breakfast and would I go up and have coffee with her, I felt almost disappointed. I said I'd be up in a minute and he left.

After Ernesto had gone I poked around. My room was long and rather narrow and had an immensely high ceiling. Against one whitewashed wall was a bed and on either side of that were doors. On inspection, one door turned out to lead to a toilet, the other to a passageway that led across the archway over one side of the courtyard and into the tiny balcony of the chapel. I came back into the bedroom. At the other end were a bureau and a desk on either side of an enormous fireplace. There was a washstand and, opposite, up one step, a huge window with tall shutters opening in. Since it was still morning and cool, the shutters were open. I stepped up and leaned out, noticing as I did so that the walls were at least three feet thick. Back in 1409, which was when the castle was built, walls were constructed to withstand siege.

Out in the courtyard the *fattore,* Signore Ottiani, was getting into his Volks. Castle Cat was playing a running and pouncing game with a cellophane ball. Above me, from the kitchen, Lucia's voice came in bursts and volleys. A pickup truck with sacks of grain was just coming under one of the archways into the yard. It was a warm, friendly scene. Yet I felt remote from it. I felt even more remote when I stepped back into the room, which had a still, almost eerie quality, as though too much time had passed through it.

Going back through the halls, I went up two flights of stairs and onto the second floor, which was much more modern, having been built early in the nineteenth century, and to which the twentieth century had (blessedly) contributed several bathrooms. At the end of a wide hall flagged with red tiles was the dining room. As I approached, I could see Sylvia at the head of the table.

"Come in, Meg dear," she said. "Sit down and have some coffee. Do you know everyone?"

"Everyone" seemed, at the moment, to consist of three Chadwicks—Mark's wife Pat, Robert, aged eight and Betty, aged six—my father and two elderly ladies.

"Go get yourself some coffee and come sit here," Sylvia said, indicating a place on her left. Opposite, on her right, was my father.

I got some coffee and hot milk from the kitchen and

93

came back to sit at the dining table. At my back were two French windows leading out to small balconies, so that the morning light, pouring in, was on Father's face. This morning he had on a blue shirt open at the neck and a light jacket. It was funny to see my own face in male form and in its forties. Before, when I was with him, either I was beside him or, since I was so much shorter, below him. And, anyway, I had been too shy to look at him very much. Now, our heads were on a level. Father was occupied talking to Sylvia, and I stared unabashedly. His nose, besides being long and tilted at the end, was crooked. There was a scar on his upper lip. I had always imagined clergy with mouths like down-turned semicircles as on the people in that painting, *American Gothic*. It was therefore, I mused, interesting to see that Father's mouth was fuller and indented in the corners, also like mine. In fact—

"Do I have a smut on my nose or egg on my chin?" Father asked.

I could feel myself blushing. "Sorry. I was staring."

"It's all right."

But I could tell it wasn't. With one hand he was nervously rolling up crumbs beside his plate.

"After all," I said, "I've never seen you before." The minute I said that I remembered that it was Mother's fault, not his.

My words fell into one of those silences.

Pat Chadwick stood up. "Robert, Betty, it's time we made our beds and did our wash."

"I want to swim!" her offspring shouted in chorus.

94

"*After* beds are made," Pat said with the loving firmness I found so admirable. Taking a reluctant hand in each of hers she shepherded them to the door. The two elderly ladies, muttering to each other in French, rose and moved majestically to a door at the other end of the big dining room.

"I'm taking Denise and Cecile to Assisi today," Sylvia said. "Do you want to come?"

One of Father's eyebrows went up. He looked at me. "Meg?"

"Yes," I said immediately, "I'd love to," glad of an outing *en masse* so that Father and I would not be alone together.

It was a strange week, filled with light and dark, and I remember it as a series of stills, or isolated scenes.

There was, as we drove along the main road, that first sight of Assisi, which, no matter how many times I approached it, still gave me goose bumps. Rising above the plain like some kind of mirage, it soared up the hill to the ruined fortress at the top.

As we neared the place in the road where Assisi seemed to materialize, suddenly, halfway up to the sky, neither Sylvia nor I said anything: I because I was inclined (snobbishly) to mark people on their instant reactions, Sylvia possibly for the same reason—more likely because she was wondering how much exercise she should subject her elderly guests to. The latter, still talking French to each other in the back seat of the station wagon, missed the moment. But beside me I heard Father's sudden intake of breath. I waited to see if he would make some banal comment. But he didn't. Half grudgingly, half pleased, I gave him full marks.

There was the moment when we went into the Basilica of St. Francis, weaving our way through clumps of German, French, American, English, Spanish and (I think) Swedish tourists, all with their guides, all talking in full voice. We went down to the crypt. We went up to the upper church and looked at the Giottos. Father stared at the famous frescoes. "They seem awfully bright to be nearly seven centuries old," he said tentatively.

"Peter says they're touched up."

"I can believe it."

"Do you like them?"

He glanced around and then down at me. "Truthfully, I don't have any reaction at all. My wife tells me I'm a visual idiot."

My heart gave an odd skip. "Your wife?" Why hadn't I realized that of course by now he would be married again?

"Yes. She sculpts a little when she has time."

"I suppose she's very busy, being a minister's wife and all."

"No. Yes. That is, she *is* busy—extremely so. But not running the women's guild, if that's what you're thinking. She's a doctor."

"Oh."

We started to walk out of the upper church.

Sylvia had parked the car and announced that she was

going to escort the ladies herself and give them lunch and we could meet her back below the basilica at three thirty. Since being left alone with Father was not what I had planned I had given her a reproachful look.

"I'm sorry, dear," Sylvia had said quietly but briskly as she got her ticket from the man in charge of the parking. "But Denise and Cecile are old, arthritic and they know no English. If we're all together, either they'll feel isolated and will talk only to each other and will miss everything, or I'll find myself translating every blessed thing you and your father say, which will be most tedious."

So Father and I were on our own. We stood at the entrance of the huge church which is almost at the foot of the town and looked up. At the thought that there were nearly four hours ahead of us, my heart sank. Well, I told myself, there were plenty of sights to keep us busy.

"What would you like to see?" I asked.

"Why don't we just walk for a while?"

"You don't want to see anything special?"

"Not at the moment."

"Well, walking in Assisi means climbing. It's practically perpendicular."

"I can see that. I should have brought my climbing boots and pitons. Do you mind climbing?"

"No. Not a bit."

"All right, then. *Andiamo*."

After we had been climbing up the narrow main street for about ten minutes, Father suddenly said, "Relax, Meg. We don't have to talk. You don't have to entertain me. I don't mind silences. I like walking through a place and getting the feel of it. I'd rather do that than rush around the official sights."

I was surprised, mostly at his perception, and then wondered why I should be.

At one point we passed a small doorway, open, but shielded from the street by curtains. "There's a chapel in there," I said. "It's very small. I've been in it a lot of times this year and last, and every time I've been there there's a girl, very young, not much older than me, with long braids and wearing a sort of veil on top. She's always there, no matter what time I've gone in, kneeling in the front pew. She never moves."

"Maybe she's a postulant of some kind of contemplative order."

"Yes, I suppose so."

"And you find that hard to understand?"

"Yes. Don't you?"

"No. Not really. Although I'm not sure I could do it myself. But, after all, people in the Eastern disciplines sit in meditation for hours. It's the same general principle. Why are you looking at me like that?"

"I keep forgetting you're a clergyman."

"You talk about it as though it were some rare and vaguely repellent disease, not often mentioned in polite society."

I giggled a little. He smiled and took my hand and, before I realized what I was doing, I squeezed his, and we walked hand in hand up to the central piazza. *I wonder what Mother would think,* I pondered, as we came to a stop. And at the thought of Mother I withdrew my hand.

"What's that?" Father asked, pointing to a decrepit piece of Roman architecture.

"It was a Roman temple to Minerva. Inside they've built a hideous church."

"It looks ready to fall down."

It did. The columns were chipped, cracked and dirty.

"Let's go in," Father said.

"I told you. It's ugly."

"You've aroused my curiosity."

"All right."

Just before we started up the steps, a small figure in a black cassock and flat shovel hat bounced up the stairs, through the doors and into the church.

When we got in Father looked around. "You were absolutely right," he said. The altar was a mass of fat pink angels, a fat pink madonna and acres of white paper lace.

"I told you," I said.

At that point a single male voice started to sing. Father and I turned. His shovel hat on the wicker chair beside him, the little priest was sitting in the front row of chairs, his face upturned to the (to me) revolting madonna, and he was singing a song in Latin. His cheeks were pink and his eyes shone. There was something almost spellbinding about his total unself-consciousness. When he was finished he paused, then started the same tune again, this time with words in

German. Then he just sat there. Father and I tiptoed out, but I had a feeling that if we had stamped all the way to the door the priest wouldn't have paid any attention.

"I liked that," Father said when we got outside. "It was nice. And I envy him."

"Why?"

"Because he was so obviously indifferent to what you and I thought. He was being himself with no effort at all. It's a great gift."

I thought about that as we stepped down into the piazza. "You know, singing to the Virgin is not Mother's thing, but if it were, she'd do it without caring what anybody thought." I could hear the defensive edge to my voice and waited for him to argue with me.

"Yes. You're right. That was always one of her most lovable qualities."

Before I could stop myself words were tumbling out of my mouth. "Then why did you leave her?"

He turned. Perhaps it was the intense, unshaded heat of the piazza, but his lips looked white. "You forget," he said gently. "She left me."

I knew I was wrong, yet I couldn't stop myself. "But you—and your mother—were arrogant and snobbish and made her feel inferior, that the Grants were something superior and special, and everything she did was wrong." Clear in my mind was the episode of the teacup and others like it that Mother had told me about, and I waited to produce them as evidence when Father would start to protest.

But he didn't. He just said, "I'm afraid you're right, Meg. We weren't very nice to her."

I waited for him to say "nevertheless" or "on the other hand" or "in my defense let me say" and then tell me about Mother's lover, Tony.

What he said was, "Should we try for some lunch somewhere? It's past one and everybody seems to be making for shelter."

I looked around. Outside one of the restaurants on the piazza the dozen or so tables under the awning were filled. The brown, white, gray and black cassocks that always fill the Assisi streets—to say nothing of the camera-hung tourists—had disappeared. But a perverse streak had taken hold of me. "I'm not hungry. Besides, there won't be a table left by now."

"I'm not hungry either. What happens if we just keep on walking up there?" And he waved a hand towards where the road slanted up out of the other side of the piazza.

"If we go on long enough we reach the Rocca Majore—the ruin of the fortress at the top. But it's very long and very hot."

"Well, I've seen a lot of fortresses, ruined and otherwise. Why don't we just walk along the streets?"

So we did, up and down and across and back again and down and up. And for what seemed like a long while we walked in silence. After a while we came to another piazza, above the central one. Off to the right was the Cathedral of San Rufino. "What's that?" Father asked.

"It's the Cathedral of San Rufino. You're supposed to admire its facade."

"Why?"

"It's a good example of twelfth-century architecture."

"All right. Let's go over so I can admire it."

As a matter of fact, the facade is beautiful—complicated yet simple, with its wide plain spaces, its delicate stonework, its gargoyles. "Peter says it has symmetry without being rigid, like the twelfth century. But then he practically lives in the twelfth century. He says everything's been going downhill ever since."

"I'd like to meet him," Father said.

"Well, he said he wanted to meet you. I think he wants to talk theology."

Father didn't say anything.

"I suppose," I said, "you think that's odd."

"Why should I think that's odd?"

"Because of his other profession, or didn't you know?"

"Didn't I know about what?"

"He writes porn—pornography."

After a minute Father said, "How versatile!"

"Are you being sarcastic?"

Suddenly he leaned towards me and took my arm and shook it. "Stop it, do you hear me? Stop trying to pick a fight! I know you're angry with me but I want you to tell me why, instead of taking these sideswipes. Now what is it?"

The words tumbled out of my mouth. "I know it's not your fault, Mother told me two days ago that you didn't know I existed, she'd left before you knew, but all my life I've been angry at you for not bothering to know me or see me or find out about me. And even though I know now it wasn't your fault . . . the whole thing is making Mother miserable . . . and I know she's ill . . . and I didn't want to come, only Mother made me. . . ." The silly, senseless words finally ran down.

In the road above the piazza a dog whimpered and went after a flea somewhere near his tail. A small car came gingerly down the road leading from the Rocca, its nose almost in the hot asphalt.

My father said in a dry, hard voice, "So you created a villain you could hate, and now you're upset because you're deprived of that villain. Is that it?"

The way he put it, it made no sense. Yet I knew it was true. "I suppose so."

"Well, let me give you back your villain. Your instincts were entirely right. I knew you were alive and that you were most likely my daughter. I knew about it when you were one or two years old, before your mother left for Europe. But I was too proud and too angry and too wounded and too full of self-pity to do a thing about it. And then, later, guilt was piled on top of all the other unappetizing feelings. I am just as neglectful as you thought I was and as you obviously want me to be. Now do you feel better?"

He paused, but I was too stunned and filled with jumbled feelings to say anything. His face looked white and set and the lines seemed much deeper.

He continued. "I would feel remiss about leaving you here, except that I know you know this town far better than I do. I'm tired of this silent battle, and I'm tired of being some kind of straw man that you keep knocking down. I'll meet you back at the car at three thirty."

And he strode up the all but vertical road leading to the Rocca above the town. I stared after him. As he disappeared around the first spiral bend I thought, *He'll get sunstroke.* But I didn't go after him.

Instead I went slowly down to the central piazza and stood looking at the tables outside the restaurant on the other side of the square. By now they were almost all empty. In the middle of the piazza the sun was a white glare. The newsstand, the stationer's, the pharmacy, bookstore and religious gift shop were all closed, their shutters all the way down. Carlo, who owns the restaurant, came out and wiped off a few of the tables. I walked across the square.

"*Ciao,* Carlo," I said. He was an old friend of Mother's and mine and had steered one or two lost and strayed tourists our way.

"*Ciao,* Mops," he said. Only with him it came out "Mobz."

"Can I use your phone? I'll pay you for the call."

He waved a hand indicating "help yourself" and I went into his ice cream–cum–liquor bar. His phone was off to one corner in an alcove and I went over there and sat down.

Twenty minutes later I was still sitting there, not having made the call—either call. My first impulse was to call Mother, but then I thought she might be having a nap, and, even if she weren't, what could she say? What I wanted her to say was: "Darling, forget the whole thing and come on home. We'll come and get you in the car." And maybe if I asked the right question or said the right thing she would say it. But wouldn't that be the blackmail she had been talking about?

And then there was the call to Cotton. I wanted him to say, "Don't pay any attention to your father, who is and always has been an inadequate, cold-blooded, unfeeling so-and-so. I'll come and get you immediately. And you won't have to bother with him anymore."

That was a lovely fantasy and I played with that even longer than with the one featuring Mother. The trouble was, I couldn't quite get it to drown out what Mother said about Cotton wanting to be free more than he wanted to be loved. The minute she said that, I knew it was true, because it was always the same with his popsies—which is what Mother called his girlfriends. The scenario was the same every time: Zingo across a crowded room or cocktail party, romance, Cotton appearing with some long-legged, long-haired adoring type hanging on his arm, *molto con amore* for several weeks, then Cotton turning up alone and with a hunted look, suddenly being gracious and helpful with our Goodie Packs, especially if they were in a city safely removed from his predatory ex-love, followed by earnest repudiations of entanglement on the ground that it interfered with his serious work, followed by peace for a few weeks or even months, followed by zingo across a crowded cocktail party. . . . After I had stared at this repetitive script for a bit, I left the alcove. Passing back through the bar I told Carlo I had changed my mind and bought an orangeade and a rather dried-up-looking sandwich from him. Carrying these I went outside and sat down.

Although the orangeade was sweet and synthetic it quenched my thirst, but the sandwich was even worse than it looked. I had assumed that Carlo had made it early that morning. I now revised my estimate to the previous morning. Gingerly I extracted the ham and nibbled at it. Having nowhere I could go and nothing I could do, I finally gave in to the depression that had been threatening to sit down on me since Father had walked off. No matter how I looked at it I had behaved badly, and he was quite right, I had been trying to pick a fight with him. I finished the ham and looked at the bread, which had now curled all around at the edges. And for no reason at all that made any sense I started to cry.

I wasn't aware that anyone was around until it finally dawned on my consciousness that the heat of the sun had suddenly been removed. For some inexplicable reason I seemed to be in the shade. I took my face out of my handkerchief and looked straight into a pale blue shirt. Then I looked up. There was Father, not two feet away, looking down at me.

He held out his hand. "I'm sorry. Forgive me. Please."

Without thinking, I took his hand and nodded.

He sat down. "I could explain about my feeling guilty, hence my temper tantrum, but somehow I'd rather we'd just forget about the whole thing. How do you feel about it?"

I felt relieved, and told him so. I found I didn't want to do any more probing and analyzing.

Carlo, scenting a new customer, ambled out and over. Father looked at the remains of my sandwich. "Did that taste as awful as it looks?"

"Worse. Carlo, I bet you made that yesterday."

Carlo looked for a moment as though he were going to deny the whole thing. Then he grinned, shrugged and laughed.

"Well," Father said, "there's not too much that you can do to ice cream. Two ice creams and two coffees."

After they had come and we had been peacefully eating for a while I said, "I was afraid you'd get sunstroke going up to the Rocca, but you didn't have time to get there and back, did you?"

"No. I went back pretty soon to the cathedral, only you'd gone, so I came back here to the piazza, but you weren't here either. So I took that road up thataway—" he waved his arm towards a road leading up out of the opposite end of the piazza—"and found an old church I liked. I was attracted to it because it didn't have a single placard outside or in that said anyone of note had been in it, been christened in it, buried in it, converted or anything else in it. It was very old, probably thirteenth-century, but it had a modern reliquary which was beautiful, and a slit of a window with no glass through which came a branch of a tree outside. There wasn't a soul there. I liked it very much."

"St. Stephen's," I said. "Yes, I like it too. What made you go there? It's not easy to find. Just a sign down some steps saying Chiesa di San Stefano."

Father pushed away his empty ice cream dish. "I suppose I went in because of Stephen, my son."

"Oh," I said. Like the mention of his wife, the fact that he had a son came as something of a shock. "How old is he?"

"He was seven when he died two years ago."

"I'm sorry."

Father didn't say anything. But he put his hand in his inside breast pocket and pulled out a thin leather case. Inside, behind a plastic window, was the photograph of a dark-haired, thin-faced boy with large brown eyes, wearing jeans and a red T-shirt. Held in one arm was a brown and white rabbit. Propped half on his knee inside the other arm was a guinea pig. He wasn't smiling, but there was something very happy-looking about his face.

Father said, "He was retarded, not very much, but some. He got on with people though he was a little shy and didn't talk too well. But he had some kind of direct channel to everything in the animal world that walked, crawled, swam or flew. Once . . ." He stopped.

I said, "Don't, if it bothers you to talk about him."

"It still does . . . sometimes. But I'll tell you this story. Once the bishop came to preach. We never insisted that Stephen go to church, but for some reason that morning he wanted to. Anyway, the bishop was in the middle of his sermon when Stephen's pet white mouse suddenly erupted out of his pocket, jumped to the front edge of the pew, ran along and then stopped to clean his whiskers directly in front of an old lady who looked as though she were going into shock. The bishop never missed a beat. He said in a perfectly ordinary tone, 'Stephen, what is your mouse named?' I thought Steve would be frightened at this voice coming at him from the pulpit but he wasn't. He just answered, 'Francis.' Then the bishop said, 'Well, I think you'd better get up and recapture Francis before he upsets anyone.' And then he continued with his sermon while Steve got up and put Francis back in his pocket."

"Did he—did he have an accident or something?"

"No. He got meningitis." Father paused. "He was the nicest and gentlest person I've ever known. I don't know whether he learned anything from me, but I learned a great deal from him." He put the photograph back in his pocket and looked at his watch. "It's three fifteen. Hadn't we better be getting back to the car?"

5

There were some funny moments that week. The first occurred the next day, which was Sunday.

"I think," Sylvia said at breakfast, "that you should put on your round collar, Alan. Don Ludovico is coming over to say Mass in the chapel. It might show him support."

"Wouldn't he look on it as a heretic invasion?"

"Oh, no. He's quite at peace with our heresy. We all sit upstairs in the balcony except, of course, for Denise and Cecile, who are Catholic."

"Well, if I sit upstairs in the chapel I don't see why I have to put on my dog collar."

"I thought you might sit downstairs. However, don't if you'd rather not."

The bell for Mass started ringing at eleven thirty. At twenty to twelve Don Ludovico drove into the courtyard in his Volks and disappeared into the room next to the chapel. At ten to twelve he reappeared in the courtyard, arrayed in his black cassock. People from the farms had been straggling in and the Ottiani family emerged from their house, Mrs. Ottiani and her two daughters in veils. I was waiting at the bottom of the steps with the Chadwicks, preparatory to slipping back through my room and over to the chapel balcony. Suddenly, out of the corner of my eye, I saw Father emerge from the double doors of the castle behind me, a long figure in black suit, black front and round white collar. I turned and stared at him. The clothes made him seem different. Lately, perhaps because of what he had told me about Stephen, we had become more relaxed, easier with each other. But now, in this uniform, he seemed to have retreated into another self, reserved and austere.

"Is it that bad?" he asked, looking down at me.

"I'm just not used to it."

"You can blame it on Sylvia. It was her idea."

Sylvia, in black lace veil, appeared from behind him. "How like a man to say that. You haven't changed a bit since Adam."

"Adam who?" I asked, not thinking.

Father said, "She is referring to our pusillanimous ancestor."

"Oh. In what way?"

Sylvia adjusted her mantilla. "Now's your opportunity, Alan."

"Yes, well," Father said. "I'm not sure I feel up to instructing Meg in the full theology of the Fall three minutes before Mass is due to start. What Sylvia is talking about, Meg, is the Lord asking Adam, 'Hast thou eaten of the tree whereof I commanded thee that thou shouldest not eat?' And Adam, putting it squarely on Eve, 'The woman whom thou gavest to be with me, she gave me of the tree, and I did eat.' "

"I know about the snake and all that, but I've never been sure what the whole thing meant."

Sylvia gave Father a slightly malicious smile. "Well, Alan?"

"Another time."

Don Ludovico broke away from the Ottianis and came towards Sylvia, who introduced him to Father. Far from making the sign of the evil eye, which Father seemed to expect, Don Ludovico beamed and pumped Father's hand, chattering in Italian, which Sylvia translated in short spurts.

Father said, a bit anxiously, "Sylvia, how do you tell him that though I consider myself a priest of the Holy Catholic Church, I am not a priest of the *Roman* Catholic Church? Maybe you'd better tell him that Meg is my daughter."

"He can see that for himself, and I am sure it doesn't faze him. However—" And she rushed into a volley of Italian, the result of which was that Don Ludovico threw up his hands in visible delight and pumped both of Father's hands this time.

Father, reassured that he was not sailing under false colors, responded with a warm smile. Don Ludovico, who came up to just below his shoulder, patted him on the back. Father returned the gesture. Then they wandered off a few steps in great amity.

"Whatever you said, it was right," I said to Sylvia.

"Yes, well, Don Ludovico has never seen a Protestant clergyman before and he couldn't be more delighted. I think the Chadwicks and I had better repair to the balcony."

"Where are Denise and Cecile?"

"They've been in the chapel for half an hour. Meg dear, you may come with us if you wish, but I think your father would very much like to have you sit with him."

I was about to refuse when Father, turning from Don Ludovico, said rather tentatively to me, "I don't suppose you'd like to sit downstairs with me?"

"All right," I said, a little surprised at myself.

Most of the people attending, I noticed when I walked in with Father, were standing. There were six pews, built rather high above the marble floors. Denise and Cecile occupied one. The other five were empty.

Father and I had taken up our stations at the back when there was a sort of hissing from the balcony. Father stepped forward and looked up.

"Sit in the pew," Sylvia whispered, craning over and pointing to the other front one across from the French ladies.

"What about all the other people?" Father whispered back.

"They're perfectly welcome to use the pews, though they never do. But they would think it odd and rude if you didn't."

So Father and I climbed into the ancient, creaking pew. A bell rang and Don Ludovico came in, followed by two very small boys in very short shorts. One of them I recognized as Dominici, grandson of Lucia and Ernesto, and what my mother, in one of her more Alabama fits, called a limb of Satan. But this was mostly because he gave her the sign of the evil eye one day when she reproached him for throwing stones at Castle Cat, who was up in a tree and quite determined not to come down.

The Mass was rather dull and I was beginning to doze off when a diversion occurred. Castle Cat, a rangy half-grown tom with an inquiring disposition, wandered into the sanctuary from the anteroom. Discovering the folds of altar cloth lying on the top step, he pretended they were an ambush and pounced. One of the little altar boys giggled and proceeded to give chase. The cat ran up the altar cloth, across the altar and down. By this time Dominici, also giggling, had approached it from the other side. Don Ludovico, absorbed in reading the Gospel, paid no attention. The cat, entering into the spirit of the game, avoided both boys by leaping over their outstretched hands to the floor of the sanctuary. From there it jumped up to the base of a statue of St. Catherine of Siena and tore around as the boys closed in. On the way it managed to unsettle two candles, which tottered for a minute. There was a gasp and muffled laughs from the congregation. Don Ludovico stoically read on, unmoved by the disturbances going on behind him. Forced to leave the statue, the cat soared over the boys' heads and landed again on the floor of the sanctuary, at which point it discovered Don Ludovico's cassock and ran up it for about a foot. Don Ludovico never missed a syllable, though one hand crept down and gave the cassock a shake, trying to dislodge the intruder. The cat jumped off and jumped on at another angle. Don Ludovico, still reading, gave his cassock another gentle shake. The boys closed in on the cat, who evaded them, jumped over the priest's arm and, out of sight behind him for a few seconds, suddenly appeared on his shoulder.

At this point my father, who had been staring, rapt, stood up, strode over and gently removed the cat before it could jump again. Then, carrying it back through the small chapel, he put it outside and shut the door.

"You spoiled the cat's fun," I whispered.

"Yes. I know. But my sympathy was with Don Ludovico. He was magnificent. I couldn't have read the Gospel over such distraction."

The only acknowledgment by the priest of the little drama was a slight, barely visible smile in Father's direction.

Then there was the plump lady writer who turned up the next morning. Sylvia put her in a single room off the dining room. Two mornings later Father, Sylvia and I were having a discussion in the hall outside the dining room after breakfast when the writer, a Miss Huggins, suddenly appeared, clad in a blue kimono and an alarmed expression.

"Sylvia, there's a scorpion—"

Unfortunately for her, Ernesto, followed by Mr. Ottiani, came up the stairs at that moment and, not hearing Miss Huggins, plunged into an excited account of a break in one of the water pipes leading from the lake. Sylvia, who had lived through more than one water crisis with twelve guests and no water at all, turned her full attention to the two men. Miss Huggins, who did not speak Italian, did not understand what they were saying and she was plainly suffering a crisis of her own that she considered equally important. The antiphonal chorus in Italian and English proceeded:

"Signorina Matthews, there's a break in a pipe down near Francesco's farm . . ."

"Sylvia, I don't want to be a bother, but there's a scorpion . . ."

"The plumber is afraid it may take a while . . ."

". . . in the bath, I poured water over it three times . . ."

"The water to the castle may have to be cut off . . ."

". . . but it crawled right back up again . . ."

". . . the farms have first priority with the crops and the cattle, and . . ."

"I don't wish to make a fuss, but . . ."

"If we cut the water off now, we can reinstate . . ."

". . . all God's creatures, I know, but . . ."

". . . no baths for the rest of the day . . ."

". . . I can't seem to apply it to scorpions . . ."

"Lisa, be *quiet!*" Sylvia, who could be alarmingly like a field marshal in moments of urgency, turned back to the men, decided in favor of cutting the water off within an hour in the hope that it could be restored by late afternoon, then gave her attention to Miss Huggins, who looked both stubborn and wounded. "I'm sorry, Lisa dear, but water here comes before anything. Now what are you trying to tell me?"

Miss Huggins tightened her kimono around her and said with a note of grievance, "There's a LARGE scorpion in my bathtub."

"Well, why didn't you pick it up with a piece of paper and put it down the toilet?" Sylvia, brought up by a naturalist father, had little sympathy with squeamishness over phenomena such as scorpions, millipedes and bats, all of which invaded the castle and gave sensitive guests the jitters.

"Pick it up?" Miss Huggins's voice rose in alarm.

"Never mind, dear. I'll show you."

By this time most of the guests, wandering through the hall either to or from breakfast, had stopped and were enjoying the show.

"May I have the scorpion for my collection?" Robert Chadwick asked.

"Not this time, Robert. I wish to show Miss Huggins how to put it down the toilet." And Sylvia moved briskly off into the dining room with her guests following like a caravan train. We went through Miss Huggins's small room to her bathroom, built in one of the round towers at the

117

corner of the castle. Sure enough, in the white porcelain bathtub was a black triangular shape, its tail waving angrily.

"It's *not* a *large* scorpion," Sylvia said with some indignation. "However," she went on, conceding a point, "it *is* a scorpion. Lisa, bring me a piece of your writing paper."

Miss Huggins shuffled off in her mules and was back with a piece of her stationery. Sylvia poked one corner of this at the scorpion, who promptly climbed on the paper. Taking him over to the toilet, she shook him in and then pulled the lever. "I don't think he can come up from that," she said.

"Are you *sure?*" Miss Huggins said.

"No, but just keep this paper here and you can shake him down again, or out the window, although probably he'd just land on the wall and crawl up again. Jennie, who occupied your room last week, found one on her bed one afternoon. Lisa, are you all right, dear? Perhaps you'd better sit down. You know, if you just keep the bed away from the wall and don't let any bedclothes trail to the floor, you won't have anything to worry about . . ."

Father and I left the scene where Miss Huggins was getting whiter by the minute. "Poor Miss Huggins will never take another bath here or sit down on the toilet. She'll probably leave on the next train," I said, and repeated this to Sylvia who joined us in the sitting room.

"Nonsense," Sylvia said. "If you don't want wildlife, you shouldn't come into the country."

"How about ghosts?" somebody asked. "After all, how old is this place?"

"Nearly six hundred years. Three people have seen or heard things, but I never have. I don't think I'm particularly sensitive." Sylvia took an English pride in her lack of sensitivity.

But her answer bothered me a little, because I had not been sleeping well.

My bed, which was old, as was the lumpy mattress, was not comfortable, but I had slept in literally hundreds of beds, most of them just as uncomfortable. It was hot, but then it was even hotter in Maria's apartment in Perugia, and I had slept very well indeed there on the sofa.

But each night I had been at the castle I had been unable to fall asleep until almost dawn. Since I don't need much sleep, this hadn't bothered me too greatly. And, for some reason, I was reluctant to admit it or talk about it. I put it down to worry about Mother, but I had been worried about her in Perugia also, and although I had sometimes waked up in the night, I had not, night after night, been unable to fall asleep. The trouble with lying awake was that if I turned on the bedside light, the room could be, and twice was, invaded by a bat, which swooped around and around swinging lower and lower. I had no particular aversion to bats. On the other hand, I didn't want it to hit me so all I could do was to turn off the light and wait for the bat to find its way out. To get up and close the shutters while I read made the room stuffy. And if I read myself sleepy, then I woke myself up when I got up again to open the shutters after I had turned off the light. So what with one thing and another, I had not slept much, and had had to make it up in siestas after lunch.

On the night after the question about ghosts I didn't go to sleep at all. As I lay there, squirming about, trying to get cool, I pondered the question about ghosts again. With the morning light streaking into the sitting room my answer would have been, *No, I do not believe in ghosts.* Now, at night, as I lay alone, the sole occupant of the huge first floor, my answer might . . . would . . . have been different. Mother and I had lived in an awful lot of pensions, boarding houses, small hotels, the homes and studios of friends, as Mother and Peter had got one job or another, here and there, ranging from Holland in the north to Italy in the south with side stops in Switzerland, Germany and Austria. Mother had worked for travel agents, shoestring tours and small hotels that needed gimmicks to attract tourists. We had lived from hand to mouth. My education was, to say the least, slapdash. But it had been fun, even if a little suspenseful when bill time came. And as a result of lack of space, I had seldom slept alone. Frequently Mother, Peter and I slept in one room, Mother and Peter in the beds and me on a couch with a blanket strung between, or Mother and me in bed and Peter on the couch, or Mother and me in bed and Peter rolled in a blanket on the floor. I had never had many friends of my own age, except that Mother, Peter and, when he was with us, Cotton and I seemed the same age. So I never felt lonely or alone.

Now I was alone. A hundred empty yards of stone and tile spread around my room. Everyone else was twenty feet above me, and through heaven knew how many thicknesses of stone.

"You don't mind being down there alone?" Sylvia had asked kindly, when I arrived. And I had said, "No," because I had not yet slept there alone. Now I did mind. But I didn't know what to do about it. Every bed upstairs was taken. Father, I knew, occupied a room off the sitting room which he had shared for one or two nights with an elderly Hungarian professor, who had since left.

Matters came to a head two nights after Miss Huggins's encounter with the scorpion, aided, I think, by a trip Father and I had made that day to a deserted Benedictine monastery at the base of a nearby mountain.

Technically speaking, it wasn't deserted. The land and the farm buildings attached to the property had been taken over by the Ministry of Agriculture, which had installed a laboratory there and carried out various experiments with the crops and soil. One or two old monks remained and lived in one small portion of what had been the cloister and said Mass in the ancient crypt of the church, which was pre-thirteenth-century and therefore visited by tourists and mediaeval scholars. It was, in Mother's parlance, a Tiddle-de-pom, a short foray, which was why Father and I went one day around five, driving in Sylvia's car.

After we had admired the outside and talked to one of the monks, we went into the upper church, now abandoned, to go downstairs into the crypt. I had been there before, of course, but we had always just sped through on the way to the stairs. This time Father and I loitered. What remained of decoration and paintings upstairs were in the worst rococo tradition.

"Awful," I said, turning around. And then I saw it, in a glass case, under an enormous and hideous painting of the Romantic period.

Skeletons and the blackened bodies of saints are no great rarity in this part of Italy. There is the body of St. Clare in Assisi, black as ebony, carefully tended by the nuns. In Gubbio, high above the altar of the Church of St. Ubaldo, is the saint's body, also black, preserved as a sacred relic. Occasionally tourists, sometimes English, often American, got a little white about the gills when confronted with these monuments to relic piety and the casual acceptance of death, and Mother, in her more mischievous moods, would not give advance warning, to see the effect on Western middle-class sensibilities. I had always thought it was fun.

Now I didn't. The skeleton lay there in the half-open glass case, a dried-up garland of what were still identifiable as flowers sagging rakishly over the skull, wisps and rags of disintegrated silk lying around him (her?)—definitely, I thought, with the garland, her. And with that it stopped being faintly comic and meaningless and became a body that had once worn flesh and walked upright and had eyes and a mouth and laughed, like my mother, who sometimes, when we were on picnics, picked flowers and leaves and made garlands of them for her head. A chill like a thousand ages of blackness and ice came over me.

"Are you coming?" Father called, halfway down to the crypt.

"Yes," I said, and walked slowly after him.

That evening, to my relief, Father's things were moved down to the first floor, to a double room on the other side of the banqueting hall. A family consisting of two parents and two children was due to arrive, and Sylvia, playing around with rooms and spaces and families and people who could be divided up and those who couldn't, decided to put the whole group in the two rooms off the sitting room.

"You don't mind, Alan, do you? Actually, you'll have a bathroom to yourself, and Meg across the hall."

"Not at all," Father said with a smile at me. "My pleasure."

That night, aware of another human being on the same floor, I went to sleep almost immediately. The trouble was, I dreamed about the skeleton. It was lying there, with the remnants of the silk and the flowers, just as it had that afternoon, when suddenly Mother, in her yellow dress, started to climb out of the glass case, only the opening wasn't large enough and she was stuck and crying out to me. . . .

I woke up with my heart pounding. The moon must have set because I could barely tell the difference between the black of the room's interior and the outside. "Mother," I said aloud.

There was the sound of something running across the

floor, and terror came down on me. For a while I lay there, fighting it. Then, forcing myself, I reached out and turned on the light. A mouse scampered across the floor and behind the wardrobe. There was the sound of wings and a bat flew through the window. With a sob I plunged out of bed and up and across the room to the door, which I wrenched open and then closed behind me.

The stone beneath my feet was cold. A faint light from stars came through the window, high up in the wall of the great room. Down where I was, it was black. And suddenly I was afraid of everything: of the scorpions that at this time of year did indeed come into the castle and rest on the stone floors, of the mice that ran around, of the skeleton that I couldn't get out of my head, of my dream with Mother trying to get out of her tomb. I wanted to scream and cry out. But I managed not to, and, sliding my feet across the floor, succeeded in getting to a wall where I knew there was a light switch. Finding it, I turned it on, then ran across the hall to the door opposite and pounded on it. "Father," I called, too preoccupied to realize that that was the first time I had used that name. "Father!"

He came to the door, knotting the cord of his robe.

"Meg, what's the matter?"

I didn't know where to begin. "I'm afraid," was all I managed to get out, because I was shivering.

"You're also cold. Here." He drew me into the room and pulled the quilt from the unused twin bed. "Put this around you," and he did it for me. "Now," he said kindly, leading me over to the bed, gently pushing me down and sitting beside me. "What's the matter? Tell me about it."

"I had a dream about the skeleton. I'm scared Mother's going to die." And I started to cry.

He didn't say anything at all. Just held me and rubbed my back. After a while I said, "Do you think Mother's going to die? Do you think that's why she wrote you?"

"I don't know, Meg. But I suspect, somehow, that it's a possibility."

So, wrapped in the quilt, leaning against Father, I confronted it for the first time, and the pain was like somebody putting their hands inside me and tearing me apart.

"I want to go home," I said.

"All right. I'll take you home tomorrow. What do you call home?"

"Mother," I said. "She's home, wherever she is."

After a while Father said, "Would you like to sleep in here with me, in this bed?"

"Yes," I said. "I hate it in there."

So I took off the quilt and got into the bed, and Father turned off the bedside light. Then I heard him go across the room, throw his robe over a chair and get into the other bed.

We lay there in the dark for a while. Then Father said, "I wish there were something I could say or do that would make you feel better, but I can't think of anything."

"Why should you?" I asked. I felt as though I were lying under layers of pain and fear.

"Well, it's supposed to be part of a priest's stock in trade."

125

"Oh." I had completely forgotten that he was a clergyman. I shifted the enormous burden of Mother and what might be happening to her away a little. "What made you become a priest? Was it a sudden conversion or something?"

"No . . . no, I don't think so."

"You know, Mother—" The pain came back as I said the word. "Mother didn't say a word about your being in the Church. She never said exactly what you did, but I got the idea it was in a bank or brokerage house. Something terribly respectable . . . that people who have long family trees and lots of money do."

"Ouch!"

"Did I say something wrong?"

"No, something accurate. I was in the army when we met and married. But my stint in the service was over before the Vietnam war escalated, and during the rest of our brief marriage I was connected with a brokerage house. I didn't go into the Church until several years after . . . after the divorce."

"Is it all right, your being divorced? With the Church, I mean?"

"I wouldn't say it was all right, exactly. But we . . . we were not married in church. We eloped and were married by a judge. And that and the divorce were long before I was ordained. So after putting it through the hierarchy two or three times and looking at it, the bishop decided it was okay."

"Why did you elope?"

Father didn't say anything for a minute.

"Was it because of your mother?" I persisted.

"Yes. I'm afraid so. I don't blame her. She herself was a product of a certain outmoded way of looking at things. Also, it always came as a shock to her that she couldn't have her own way in everything. But I do blame myself. I came of a younger generation. I was in the army. I knew the world wasn't the way she thought it was. When I told her I wanted to marry your mother, she raised all kinds of objections. I should have stood still and insisted on doing it up as properly and full of ceremony as though I were marrying a girl she had picked out for me. But I didn't have the intestinal fortitude to do that. Instead, I induced your mother to run away with me."

"Well, from your point of view, isn't it just as well you did? I mean, if it had been done in a church, you couldn't now be a priest, could you?"

Father was silent for a while. Then he said, "I've thought about that a lot, Meg. One answer is, of course, that you're right. But there's another answer and I'm not at all sure it isn't the truer one. If I had stood my ground as I should have, then the marriage might have been different."

"But Mother said she . . . she had an affair with somebody named Tony and ran away because you were jealous. She said . . ." I hunted around for her exact expression, "that you wouldn't let her be both free and loved."

"Yes, I know. But I have never been sure, and I don't suppose I now ever will be, whether my jealousy and

127

possessiveness wasn't so much noise to cover the fact that somewhere in my depths I knew I had let her down."

We didn't talk for a while. I lay there wishing that sleep, like an anesthetic, would come. But even though I did not feel so alone, sleep was still far away. Finally I said, "What's your present wife like? What's her name?"

"Rachel. Her name, before we were married, was Rachel Levy. She is of Jewish, though nonreligious, background."

"Didn't your mother object?"

"She certainly did. But this time I was married before the altar of the Church and told Mother that if she wanted to attend she would be welcome, and if she didn't, that would be all right, too. And I learned a lesson then about would-be tyrants. I didn't expect to see her at my wedding. But when I came in with my best man, there she was, sitting in the front pew, handkerchief at the ready. And she cried all the way through, just like any other mother."

"Was she nice to Rachel afterwards?"

"Yes, because Rachel called her bluff. After we got back from the wedding trip Rachel, without telling me, called on Mother in her apartment and said, before Mother could strike an attitude, 'Now shall we be friends or not? I'd like it, but it's up to you.' And Mother was so flummoxed she said 'Friends' and afterwards couldn't back down. And then, after Stephen was born, and we discovered that he wasn't . . . entirely normal, she came through marvelously. She'd always been good with little boys, and she and

Stephen became great friends. Of course, I don't see how anybody could not be friends with Stephen. . . ."

I thought about Stephen, who had died, and about Mother, who might die. "Father, how did you bear it, when Stephen died? What did you do . . . ?"

"You asked me what made me go into the Church. I was very angry and bitter when your mother ran away—although I want you to know that now I don't blame her at all. At least she had the guts to take action, which I didn't, but it took me a long time to see it. Anyway, along with blaming your mother, I blamed mine, and so, like the child I was, I refused to do a whole lot of things she liked me to do, or wanted to do with me, which included going to our family church. I stayed that way for a few years, feeling sorry for myself, treating myself to various excesses to make up for the dirty hand fate had dealt me, and so on. . . .

"Among other things I didn't bother to do was work very hard. The firm I was with was family—my grandfather had founded it, so my turning up late and leaving early and coming back from lunch not exactly sober was excused. The partners looked the other way . . . Poor Alan, who can blame him for going to the dogs? Such a raw deal . . . and so on. I knew that was the way they were arguing to themselves, and I took full advantage of it. Then one day a guy who was a customer of mine was wiped out as a result of my carelessness. I knew I should have gotten his money out of a particular fund. More than one hint had been dropped. But I kept putting it off. . . . He didn't jump out of the window or anything. But he did have a car accident that turned out to be fatal both for him and for the guy he ran into. Drunk while driving. . . . So then I went to the other extreme—it was all my fault, and that gave me all the excuse I needed to do some more commiserating with myself. Finally, the firm, family or no family, fired me, and when they did so they told me it would have been a favor to me and to heaven knows how many of their customers if they had done so long since. . . . So for a while I did nothing at all, professionally, that is.

"Then, one Sunday morning when Mother was up at the Cape, I wandered into church—not the one the family had always gone to, but another one. Anyway, it's hard to describe, because nothing dramatic happened. It was ordinary Morning Prayer. At the usual moment everybody got up to sing the psalm. It was the regular liturgical music, but it was loud and vigorous and people sang well, and I felt as though it broke over me in a huge wave that had started back down the centuries at the beginnings of the Church. Then a layman got up to read from the Old Testament, from Jeremiah. I must have heard what he read hundreds of times before without really listening. But this time I listened and what hit my ear were the words: *I have loved thee with an everlasting love.* . . . And there, in the pew by myself, with people all around, I started to cry.

"You asked me what I thought or did when Stephen died. That's what I held onto, because I believed it to be true, and, if it were true, then I had nothing to fear for

Stephen, or even myself, even though I missed him so much. . . ."

Neither of us said anything after that, and after a while I went to sleep.

The next day Father borrowed Sylvia's car and drove me back to Maria's apartment. When he pulled up outside he said, "I'll be leaving for Rome tomorrow, Meg. So this is goodbye for the time being."

"Do you want to come in?"

He hesitated. "No. Not this time. Give her my love, Meg. And tell her—" He paused.

"Tell her what?"

He flicked my cheek with his finger. "That she's done a good job."

"Thanks," I said.

He smiled. "You're welcome." Then he leaned over and kissed my cheek. *"Arrivederci."*

6

The Pride—Mother, Peter, Cotton and I—had one more glorious picnic. Peter, who collected monasteries the way fans collect autographs, had heard of an old Benedictine monastery at the top of a mountain near Civitella. Apparently it had been in continuous use from about 1300 to World War II, when the few remaining elderly monks had died off.

"Would you like to go, darling?" Mother had asked from her sofa in Maria's sitting room. It was still hot outside, but Mother had a shawl over her and a quilt on her feet.

One of her tent dresses camouflaged her from the neck down, but her face was very thin and drawn.

"It would involve some climbing." Peter sounded doubtful.

"Then let's go. I can climb," Mother said. And then added, "Please."

I'll never forget that day. It was the last of the hot weather before the summer broke. The sky was an intense blue. Cotton, who was driving, turned the car around and around the long hairpin loops going up the mountain. At a certain height the round hills seemed suddenly to be filled with clump after clump of waving broom, the yellow of its flower brilliant against the blue of the sky.

Finally the road, which by this time was nothing but a track, ended at a small lake. Cotton parked there and took out the picnic basket. We sat on the scrub and grass and nibbled sandwiches and drank wine and orange soda. Below, set in the blue green valley like a jewel, was a tiny village, a *civitella,* a minute community nestled around a solitary fortified tower.

After lunch we scrambled down and walked through it. From end to end, the little stone street was barely forty feet long. On either side huddled houses, barns and a small church of the same gray stone. All now was deserted. There were no people about. The red flame that burns by every altar in Italy was out.

"Why do you suppose they left?" Mother asked.

Peter, who was looking sadder by the minute—he

hated to see country ways and places abandoned—said, "What's to keep them now? Farming's hard work. More money to be made in the cities, and the city's what they see on the telly."

Coming back up the hill to where the car was parked was hard work for Mother. About a third of the way up she stopped.

"I'll just get my breath," she said.

But Cotton, who is tall and very strong, picked her up and carried her. "I've always wanted to do this and now's my chance," he said.

When we got up to the top Mother thanked Cotton with all her old charm and élan and then said, "Now why don't you both go and explore Peter's monastery?"

"Too puffed. Getting too fat," Peter said promptly, patting his somewhat shrunken paunch.

"No, please, I want you to," Mother said. "Meg and I'll sit here and admire the view while I get my breath back. Now GO!"

"All right, all right," Peter muttered. The two men strode up the road.

"They look like the figure 10," Mother said, watching their retreating forms. And they did, Cotton's red head atop the vertical and Peter almost circular.

"Come sit beside me, darling," Mother said.

So I went over. But before I sat down I picked up Cotton's camera and took a picture of Mother sitting there between the tall waving yellow broom stalks. She had on her yellow dress and underneath her floppy straw hat her eyes sparkled briefly as they once used to.

I snapped the picture and then went and sat beside Mother and we talked about everything and nothing for the next hour. I was very pleased with myself because twice I made her laugh: once over the cat and Don Ludovico, and the second time over Miss Huggins and the scorpion in her bathtub. Over that she laughed so hard she had to lie back among the broom reeds and hold her sides. For a moment she looked young again and filled with life and mischief. But later I had to help her sit up and the shadow that seemed now always over her returned.

The disease moved fast.

"Why didn't you tell me?" I asked the doctor one day as he emerged from one of his visits with her, which were now two and three and sometimes four a day.

He put away his syringe. "Because there was always a chance that there might be a remission." He paused. Then he said, "It has advanced more rapidly than I thought. Soon she will have to return to the hospital."

"Is there anything you can do?"

"No, not really. Just try to make it easier for her."

In the end Mother did not go to the hospital.

Maria, who said she had a lot of research to do at the museum and library in Florence, turned over the apartment to us and went and stayed in Florence with a friend. From time to time I put up my hair and drummed up a Goodie Pack and swung them around the various local sights.

"You're very young to be doing this," one woman said, eyeing me critically.

I didn't much care for her looking after my business, but I didn't say anything, more or less on Mother's principle of "Do not wake the sleeping tiger."

But the woman was not the kind to be deterred. "How old are you?" she asked in a sharp voice.

"Eighteen," I replied, and lifted my brows in a way that would not have shamed a *marchesa*.

"Well, I didn't mean to be nosy," the woman said, her blush a tribute to my success in making her think she had committed a gaffe.

"That's quite all right," I replied in a voice calculated to make her squirm.

Mother was on heavy drugs now. Her skin was sometimes yellow and sometimes a greenish white. Occasionally she seemed her old self for a few minutes and we would talk. Mostly her beautiful eyes were glazed and dull.

One day when I got home I found the doctor and Peter arguing in the hall, the doctor insisting that he be allowed to move Mother back to the hospital.

"She doesn't want to go," Peter said stubbornly, over and over again.

"I can take better care of her there," the doctor said.

"She doesn't want to go," Peter repeated. "She hated it."

"She's not going to notice now."

"I gave her my promise."

I thought Peter was quite right. Mother had hated the hospital. One day she had walked down the hall between Cotton and me. We passed a woman with half a face and another with her face grotesquely swollen. There was a man who had no legs and a tube where his chin should have been. That's why Mother didn't go out in the hall again but agitated instead to come home early.

That night I read Mother her favorite P. G. Wodehouse—Maria had a whole shelf of his books. I don't think Mother heard too much, but when she was aware of anything she liked me to be there and I think she liked the sound of my voice.

Once, when I was sitting there looking at her, I suddenly realized I was not thinking about her at all. I was thinking, *What's going to happen to me? Where will I go? Will I be allowed to stay with Cotton?* And then I was horrified at myself.

The next day Peter said to me, "There's a new bunch of tourists up at the hotel. The man called and said they had only a day and wanted to spend it in Assisi and to stop in Gubbio on the way back."

"How about a dash to Rome and a swing through Florence while they're about it?" I said. "They must have their money's worth."

"No need to get bitter," Peter replied. "And they're willing to pay."

For a minute I wanted to say, "If you'd just earn a decent living I wouldn't have to do all this pushing around of people who want to do five countries in three days." I even got as far as saying, "I wish . . ."

But I got no further, because Peter was looking at me in a way that made me realize he knew what I was thinking.

"Sorry, Meg," he said.

I went over and kissed him. He didn't respond and I suddenly saw that he was terribly upset. "Peter . . ."

"It's all right," he said. "Only please go. Now."

So I went.

The summer weather had finally broken. It was a cold rainy day and Assisi looked bleak. Most of what Mother called the religio-hideosity shops were closed for the winter. The Giottos looked like overbright picture postcards. The tourists, who needed a day in bed more than they needed culture, were cross. So was I. We came back through Gubbio, which, according to Peter, is the most perfect mediaeval town in all Italy. As our driver eased slowly through the incomparable streets with their beautiful flat-fronted houses and their carved doors, the tourists were having a fight over air schedules.

Whether it was that or the rain or something else, I don't know. But a blackness settled down over me. I knew then what that cliché about a hand squeezing the heart meant. Because something savage was gripping mine. There seemed nothing anywhere but despair. I leaned over and touched the driver. "Back to Perugia," I said. "Now. *Subito!*"

"But we haven't finished with Gubbio," a woman tourist said angrily.

It was a cardinal rule of The Pride: Never, under any circumstances, be rude to a tourist, especially not before he pays you. But I broke it.

"You weren't looking anyway," I said. "I have to get home. My mother is ill."

But I was wrong.

Mother was no longer ill. I knew when I walked through the front door, even before I saw the doctor and Cotton standing together in the hall, what had happened.

Cotton came over and put his arm around me "She died, Mops. But it was better that way. She was in terrible pain and it would have got worse."

The doctor said, "I'm sorry."

I went in and looked at Mother. Peter was sitting there beside the bed, tears pouring down his cheeks. I looked down and found it impossible to believe that this very dead, yellow white husk was the person I had always called my mother.

We had Mother's body cremated as she had requested in a will she had dictated to Peter. And then, as she had also requested, we took the ashes up to the top of Monte Subasio, and walked up where we had had the picnic. Peter gave me the small urn and said, "You do it, Meg."

I walked alone to the edge of the hill and waited to feel something dramatic and important. But I felt absolutely nothing, and the small gray particles in the metal cannister I was carrying seemed to have nothing to do with Mother. So in a minute I simply held up the urn and the wind took the ashes and in less than a second they weren't there any more. I paused for a minute, thinking I should say something, but all I could think of was, "Goodbye." So I said it and came back to where Peter and Cotton were standing.

We found a Protestant minister in Florence and had a small memorial service, during which he read bits out of something called *The Book of Common Prayer.* Sylvia and Maria and a few friends were there.

All this time I waited for some feeling to hit me. When I had arrived back at the apartment and found Peter, tears running down his cheeks, sitting beside Mother who was dead, that huge hand or vise or whatever that had closed around my insides in Gubbio seemed to lock in place. Mother didn't look like Mother. She looked old and yellow and shrunken and disgusting and dead, and as I stood there I hated her and death and myself, and that's the only feeling I had. Everything was so different I didn't even feel that she was gone. I think it was perhaps because it seemed as though she hadn't been there for a while.

Everybody cried at the service except me. But all I could think about was that body and how awful it looked and how glad I was that it was gone. I didn't tell anyone because I kept waiting to feel the way they obviously felt.

When we were coming out Sylvia said to me, "Meg, I talked on the telephone yesterday with your father. He wants me to put you on a plane to New York. I will be shutting up Civitella in a day or two and will go down to Rome with you. I shall be going on to London . . . but of course if you would like me to go to New York with you first, I'll be glad to."

That jarred me out of the numbness I was feeling. The fears for myself that had kept coming to me within the past days were now real and happening. I said quickly, "But I'm going to stay here with Co—with Peter."

Sylvia was silent for a minute. Then she said, "Well, talk to them, my dear, and call me."

Back at Maria's apartment Peter said, "Meg dear, if you'd like us to go on living here—I mean the two of us, in Perugia or Florence—well then, that would be quite all right. The only trouble is, that last book never did get off the ground . . . and there'd be rent, and how do you feel about more Goodie Packs?"

He looked so woebegone and, for him, thin. I said, "If I didn't stay with you, Peter, what would you do?"

"There's a place back in England . . . they have some really interesting manuscripts, but I'd be quite happy to stay here with you, Mops, except that Sylvia said your father wanted you back."

I looked at him. "I wonder what Mother wanted for me. Did she say anything to you?"

"Not really. I think she felt she'd let you down. She said once she'd been a bad mother."

"That's not true," I said angrily.

"No. I don't think it is either. But I think that what she meant—or at least one of the things she meant—was that she hadn't planned to die while you were still so young. In another year or so you'd have been old enough to be on your own."

"I'm old enough now."

"No, Mops. Not really."

A question had been nagging at the back of my mind. "Peter, you all but forced me to go out with those Goodies the day Mother died. Did you know she was going to die that day?"

"Yes. I thought so. And once, a few weeks ago, after she knew . . . she said she hoped you wouldn't be there. . . ." Peter was looking at me in a worried way.

"It's all right, Peter. I think I'm glad I wasn't there." Truthfully, I wasn't quite sure. Would seeing her die have been worse than seeing her body, dead? But I didn't want Peter to be fussed. "I'm going out for a while, Peter. I'll be back soon."

He nodded. "Cotton's bringing the car around five."

I knew that, but I wanted to see Cotton alone. I was afraid he might be out when I got to his studio apartment, but when I walked up the five flights and rang the bell he was there.

"Come in," he said.

His apartment is really one huge room covered almost entirely by a skylight, plus two small closets, one a bedroom and one a bath consisting of toilet, basin and shower stall. He was busy taking books, clothes, papers and other odds and ends off the floor and stashing them away in the ancient wardrobe and chest. Since I had never seen him doing such a thing before, I asked, "Why the clean-up?"

"Because Peter is coming to stay for a while, and he's even more of a slob than I am, so at least it'll be his clutter and not mine."

"If you don't watch out you'll start showing middle-class habits."

"Yes, I was thinking that." He jammed some books and an old shirt into the closet and tried to slam the door. When it flew open and the books fell out he uttered a short, pithy word and started restacking them.

"Cotton," I said. "Can I come and stay with you too?"

"No, Mops, you have to go and stay with your father."

I fought against a sort of despairing conviction that I had known he was going to say this all along. "Please, Cotton. I don't want to go to be with my father. I don't really know him. I've never been to New York—to stay, anyway. I don't know anyone there. Peter's going to be here. Why can't I? I can easily make money. There are always some tourists around. I can sleep on the floor. I can . . ."

Cotton slammed the door. It flew open again. He said another word and then came over to me and led me over to his couch and sat us down and put his arm around me. "No, Mops. It wouldn't work."

"Why not?"

"Because it just wouldn't. You'll have to take my word for it."

"But Peter said he'd be perfectly willing to stay here—in Italy—if I wanted to," I said, adapting the truth a little.

"He's lying. What he really wants to do is to go and hibernate in some monastery on an island off the coast of East Anglia. They seem to have some recently discovered treasure trove of premediaeval manuscripts. And anyway, he'd been ambling his slow way there when he ran into your mother some years ago."

"But Peter *loved* Mother. He didn't want to be a monk."

Cotton looked at me. "You know, they're not as mutually exclusive as you think, Mops. Not really. Your mother was a sort of glorious aberration in his life. When he met her he took a long detour."

"You mean he wants to be a *priest?*"

"Oh heavens, no! Peter's not that type. But he'd be quite happy as a brother, puttering around the manuscripts, working in the garden, scrubbing floors. You know, he's not a twentieth-century character at all. He doesn't know what the word 'ambition' means. If you asked him to stay here so you could be here, he'd stay because he loved your mother and is fond of you. But he'd be miserable and you'd have to support him."

"I wouldn't mind."

"Yes, you would. After a bit."

"Mother didn't."

"That was a different relationship—as you know. And she was a different person."

A raging hot resentment against Mother rose in me. Then I remembered the way she looked, dead.

"Yes, I know," I said.

He put his arm around me. "I didn't say *better*, Mops. I just said *different*."

I turned and put both my arms around Cotton. "Can I stay with you, then, please, Cotton? Please?"

"No," Cotton said. He gave me a peck on the cheek and removed my arms.

"Can I be your popsie?"

"My *what?*"

"That's what Mother and I always called your girl-friends."

"No. Certainly not." He got up and walked around. He looked as disreputable as ever, with his torn shorts and stained shirt and dirty bare feet. But there was something about him now that made me think of my father.

"You're getting very middle-class," I said.

"I *am* middle-class about some things—such as not tampering with the morals of a minor and not wanting to go to jail."

"I'll stop being a minor very soon."

"Not to me you won't."

"We could get married."

"No, Mops. No. I'm sorry, but *no*."

I remembered then what Mother had said about Cotton needing to be free, like her. The resentment in me rose a little higher.

"I hate you," I said, getting up.

145

"That's better." Cotton looked at me. "I'm sorry, Mops, but there it is. You'll have to go to your father."

I wanted very much to cry. I also wanted very much to kick him. I got up and went towards the door. "Goodbye," I said. "It's been nice knowing you."

He came over. "Don't be a spoiled brat, Meg."

We stood there while I tried to will the tears back into my eyes.

"You know," he said, "I'd like to comfort you. But I don't want you to make something out of it."

"Please comfort me," I whispered.

He smiled a little. " 'Stay me with flagons, comfort me with apples . . .' "

Then he held me and I cried against his shirt and it was very comforting. But I knew that for him there was nothing for me to make something out of.

There was one more thing I wanted to do.

I spent the last night before Sylvia and I left for Rome at Civitella. We were due to catch an afternoon train from Terontola. Ernesto was putting our bags in the car, which would then go into a local garage for the winter. It was around noon when I said to Sylvia, "I'd like to ring the bell for Mother. Do you think it would be all right? I mean, she didn't belong to the farms or the castle."

Sylvia said, "I'll ask Lucia to help you."

So Lucia and I went down and untied the bell rope in the porch of the chapel. Then she gave the rope a long pull and the bell rang out across the valley.

"Put your hands above mine," she said.

I did, and after I had pulled with her for a while she took her hands away and watched me. When she saw that I could manage, she walked back to the castle. So I tolled the bell for Mother, remembering what Sylvia had said, that it was a kind of mourning.

7

I had my sixteenth birthday the day I landed in New York and Father met me. He and Rachel had already entered me in a school and the Monday after I arrived I went there.

School was all right. Some of the things, like languages and European history and art, I knew a lot better than the other students. Some, like American history and science, I didn't know at all.

Everybody was very nice. I think they felt sorry for me. Some were envious, because they said I had lived a very glamorous life. Others, mostly grown-ups, seemed to think that I had been deprived of a proper upbringing.

But the truth was, none of it was real. At night, when I lay in bed, I was back with The Pride—with Mother and Cotton and Peter, driving all over the place, with Peter writing his porn and Cotton forever drawing and painting and running away from his popsies and Mother making us laugh.

People would say, "How do you like New York?"

And I would say, "Fine," because it was easier than saying it didn't really exist.

I wrote to Peter about once a week and to Cotton almost every day. It was Peter who wrote to me regularly. His letters were funny and warm and very like him. They didn't say anything about me or him, but were about things like how somebody he called Brother Ponderous looked when he said his prayers, or how the birds sounded when they flew at dawn over the marshes of East Anglia, or the working habits of caterpillars. And for a little while after I read them I felt almost as though I had been with him.

Cotton wrote one letter to my ten, about things like how expensive paints had become and how he hated wasting time teaching students when he was about to break through something new in his painting. I kept asking him if he had a new popsie, and he kept not answering me.

Then I didn't hear from him. So I decided that he discovered that popsies were not what he wanted; what he wanted was me. And he was simply making up his mind to come over and get me and maybe ask me to fly back with him.

The moment I thought that, I decided it must be true and I started thinking about it in practical terms. One day I went to a phone booth outside school and telephoned all the airlines going to Italy. I found that if I left one evening around six, I would be in Rome at about eight A.M. Rome time the next day and I could get a train that would get into the station at the foot of Perugia that evening and I could take a bus or even a taxi up to Cotton's apartment and be there by ten P.M.: a little more than twenty-four hours. Only it would cost around four hundred dollars. I had singles and tens and fives that Father had periodically given me, saying, "You might need some money," and I had saved them all and put them in my underwear drawer.

When I got home, I opened my underwear drawer and counted the money. Fifty-four dollars. I needed at least three hundred and fifty more.

The next morning at breakfast I said, "Father, if I needed three hundred and fifty dollars, what would be the best way to earn it?"

Father and Rachel both looked at me. We all had early breakfast together after he had celebrated Holy Communion, and before Rachel had to leave for her clinic in a place called the South Bronx.

I had allowed for the certainty that Father would ask, "Why do you want three hundred and fifty dollars?" because that is the kind of question that most people—in fact practically anybody except Mother and Peter—ask. And I was going to say "Clothes." But he didn't. He said, "But Meg, you have three hundred and fifty dollars. I told you I had put five hundred in a checking account in your name, because I didn't want you to feel too tied or dependent. All you have to do is draw it out. Weren't you listening?"

"Yes, of course. Sorry." I mumbled, because I had no memory of it at all.

Rachel just looked at me and said nothing. I hadn't really paid much attention to her. But I did recognize that she was almost as tall as I with clear, leaf brown eyes and high cheekbones. Every now and then it occurred to me that she was keeping rather in the background.

So there was really no problem at all about getting back to Perugia.

I drew out four hundred in cash and hid it with the rest in my underwear drawer. My passport was still valid. So everything was ready for when I would receive Cotton's letter telling me he couldn't live without me and was coming over for me or simply to hop on a plane and come back.

Till then I daydreamed how it would be. Peter would come back, too. I would set up a tourist guide service on more organized lines. . . . (At this moment in my fantasy I suddenly heard Mother's voice as she once had said to me, "Mops, from somewhere you have inherited a positively *Yankee* efficiency, *not* from me!") . . . Maybe, I decided, I would do it the way Mother did, off the cuff, spontaneously, as she used to explain, with a radiant smile, when Goodies grumbled about missed connections. . . .

And then I would see that dead figure on the bed and I knew The Pride would never be together again. So I shifted back to dreaming about Cotton's writing me and telling me to hop on a plane.

But the letter didn't come.

The next thing that occurred was that I stopped going to school. I hadn't been paying a great deal of attention in class lately, so one day when I didn't feel like going, I just didn't go.

Father wanted me to see a doctor. So I went, and a man who looked exactly like a tourist who had once pinched Mother when his wife wasn't looking asked me a lot of questions which I answered as well as I could, considering I wasn't listening. I thought he was silly.

All I thought about each day was the arrival of the mail. But each day the letter didn't come. The rest of the time I read and walked. People asked me out, but I didn't go because it suddenly occurred to me that Cotton might send me a cablegram and I wouldn't be there.

Then one day the letter came. Only instead of being from Italy it was from Istanbul. Cotton said that he had left the university and that he and his most recent popsie were on their way to see the Himalayas and the Vale of Kashmir and that he had sent me a present, only it was coming by surface mail and would take weeks; and that probably in a year or so he'd finish his trip around the world and would come to New York and see me, maybe.

I was alone when I got the letter. I remember leaving the brownstone rectory. The next thing I remember was looking up and seeing a lot of Oriental people and I was on a street called Mott. Then I walked some more. I went on a ferry and I looked at New York from the boat and decided that all those upended cigar boxes were quite beautiful. I wondered what Cotton would think, only of course he would now be looking at minarets with his popsie. When I got back to the city I was tired so I climbed on a bus. Then it was late afternoon and I was walking around a square with a big arch that could almost have been in Paris or Amsterdam or London. I meandered from there down a side street and found myself in an area where all the signs were in Italian. My heart gave a little jump and I went into a bakery and spoke in Italian to the little old woman who sat behind the counter. But she looked hostilely at me. When she spoke it was with a pronounced Sicilian accent. Then another woman, much younger, came out from a room at the back and said in American, "What d'ya want?"

So I left.

And I walked some more. Eventually I went back to the rectory because there was nowhere else to go. Father and Rachel were in the living room standing talking to the doctor, who still looked like the tourist who pinched Mother.

153

Father said, "Where have you been, Meg? We've been worried."

The doctor said, "You're going through a bad time, Meg. Would you like to come and stay in—er—a rest home I know of for a while?"

That jarred me. "No," I said. "I wouldn't." And then, "I'm tired. I'm going to bed."

Rachel followed me into my bedroom. She pulled Cotton's letter out of her jacket pocket. "This was on the floor, Margaret. I read it because you had left and no one knew where you were." She put it down on the dressing table.

I didn't say anything, but I was thinking that no one had ever called me Margaret and that I rather liked it.

Rachel said, "I agree with the doctor that you are having a bad time. I've left you alone because . . . well, because I didn't know you and didn't want to intrude. Perhaps I was wrong. Anyway, I'm not a psychologist or psychiatrist. I like you and respect you and if you ever want to talk, I'd be happy to listen." She paused. I still didn't say anything. I heard what she said, but it was like listening to it through cotton wadding.

Rachel continued. "For now, there's just one thing I want to say. You're not trapped. You're not helpless. You have a choice. And I think, bad as the shock of losing everything has been, you know that. I think you're strong, stronger than you know. But you don't have to work so hard at it. You can be angry or sad or grieve and it's all right. You can even ask for help—and get it." I still didn't say anything. Rachel left.

It was undoubtedly all that walking, but I slept better that night than I had in a long time, and I dreamed, only I couldn't remember the dream. But when I woke up, I felt better.

The next morning Father said, "Would you like to go back to school?"

I shook my head. I knew that sooner or later I might have to go. But not then.

Rachel said, "Would you like to come help me in the clinic? We need all the help we can get."

I stared at her and she stared back. She got up. "I'm leaving in about five minutes if you decide to go."

So I went with her. It was a noisy, messy, smelly place filled with babies of all colors. A couple of people were feeding and emptying and washing them and holding them while Rachel examined them and talked to their parents. I helped her do that, because she doesn't know much Spanish and she said it went much faster when I was there. When the parents had all gone there was a baby called Sanchez screaming its head off. Rachel and the nurse were very busy giving treatments of one kind or another. Rachel glanced over at little Sanchez. "Pick her up," she said to me.

She was very small, only a few days old. "I'm afraid I'll drop her."

"Babies are almost indestructible."

So I picked up little Sanchez and the red went out of

her face and she stopped screaming. I put her on my shoulder and turned and looked at her and started to laugh. She looked for all the world like a little old lady sucking her gums and taking in the sights of the world. I put her down. She opened her mouth. Her face went crimson. She screamed.

"She just wants to be picked up and held," I said to Rachel, who was busy listening with her stethoscope on the chest of a two-year-old boy.

"That's right," she said, turning the little boy on his stomach. "And she doesn't mind asking."

So from time to time as I helped Rachel with the other children, I would pick up little Sanchez, who turned out to have quite a grip as she hung onto my neck. I liked her. That night I was even more tired than I had been after my walk, and I fell asleep practically while I was getting into bed.

After that I went every day with Rachel to the clinic and I liked it more and more.

"What about her schooling?" Father asked Rachel one evening when I was outside the room.

"Schooling she can get any time," I heard Rachel say. "What she needs now is . . ." But at that I walked quickly away. I didn't want to hear what I needed. I liked the clinic and that was enough.

I was so tired when I got home that I ate dinner and went to bed immediately afterwards and slept. And I liked that too, because it gave me a good excuse for not going to the parties and dinners that some of the kids at school and some of Father's parishioners, refusing to be discouraged, still invited me to. When I did go people asked me polite questions about Florence and Rome and Paris and other places, and I would answer thinking about Cotton and Peter and Mother. Only the moment Mother came into my mind, I would see her as I last saw her and I would have to go through the ritual of erasing the picture.

So I didn't go out. On Sundays sometimes I'd go to church. Sometimes I'd go to art galleries. And I would wait until Monday when Rachel and I would leave for the clinic.

Then one evening when I got home Father said, "There's a present for you. I put it in your room."

So I went in and there was a huge flat package all crated in wood.

"It's a painting," I said. "I think it must be from Cotton," and I looked at the label. It was. There was a queer tingly feeling inside me.

"Would you like me to open it for you?" Father asked. "I have a crowbar."

"Yes please."

So he did, and in about fifteen minutes the package stood by itself. Father took the wooden pieces to the side of the room and came back. I pulled away the paper and set the painting on the table where the afternoon light fell on it.

She had on the yellow dress, and the tall reeds of broom waved around her shoulders where she sat, the flowers yellow against the blue of the sky. Her floppy hat was on the back of her head, and her hazel green eyes sparkled with mischief and laughter and love and . . .

I was crying and my chest was hurting, but I said, "It's good. It's very good. It's the best work he's done. He's got that special thing Mother had. . . . I never knew what to call it . . . what it was. . . ."

"It was joy," Father said. "She was filled with it, more than anyone I've ever known."

And I knew he was right. That was what Mother had. That was what she was. But something terrible was happening inside me. That horrible body I had last seen that had stayed in the front of my mind hiding everything else was gone, and what was left was knowing that Mother was dead and I would never see her again, and the pain was beyond anything I could have imagined.

I was crying and so was Father, who was holding me.

"What's happening?" I gasped. "What is it?" The tears felt like a scalding river pouring out of me.

"It's grief," Father said. "I was afraid you'd never really grieve. It's good. Go on and grieve."

So I cried and cried for what felt like a long time.

A while later when I was tired and the river had flowed itself out I said, "Father, what shall I do?"

He said, "Why, do what your mother would have you do—live your life with as much joy as you can."

I knew then that that was what Rachel had been talking about. I had a choice. And I could choose to live.

We sat there on the bed for a while. Something Father

had said to me that night at Civitella swam up in my mind.

"What was that you said about everlasting love?"

" 'I have loved thee with an everlasting love,' " he quoted.

I thought about the words. "Where does it come from?"

He smiled a little. "From the prophet Jeremiah, the third verse of the thirty-first chapter: *The Lord hath appeared of old unto me, saying, Yea, I have loved thee with an everlasting love: therefore with loving kindness have I drawn thee.*"

"Does that have anything to do with what I am feeling now?"

"Yes. In a way."

"What way?"

"Well, Meg, only you can find the answer to that question. And you'll have to go looking for it."

About the Author

Isabelle Holland was born in Basel, Switzerland, where her father, a Foreign Service officer, was Consul. When she was three years old the family moved to Guatemala City, Guatemala, and when she was seven they moved to England, near Liverpool. She came to the United States at the age of twenty to finish college at Tulane University, New Orleans. Since graduating from college, Miss Holland has worked in New York City, mainly in publishing. She is the author of several books, including *Cecily, Amanda's Choice, The Man Without a Face,* and *Heads You Win, Tails I Lose.*